Camer[...] everything she'd lost, everything she could never have again.

Worse than that, she suspected she was going to see even more of him in the future. As Simon's surgeon, he would be overseeing his progress and Jessie would be tasked with helping the boy walk again. She cared too much to abandon the child simply because of her own discomfort around her childhood sweetheart.

Although she was probably nothing but a footnote in Cameron's story now that he appeared to be a successful, married surgeon, her highlight reel had begun and ended with him. He was the only man she'd ever loved, ever dared to plan a future with. Now it seemed she was going to have to pay the price for her mistakes again by seeing him on a regular basis.

Dear Reader,

The only thing better than our first love is reuniting with them. I speak from experience. Sometimes the timing isn't quite right, or we're not yet the people we need to be. However, I'm a great believer in soulmates, and if something is meant to be, time and distance don't matter.

Jessie and Cameron are just such a couple—teenagers who fell in love and thought they'd be together forever. Only for circumstances to bring their plans crashing down around them.

Now, fifteen years later, they meet again, forced to work together to help a young patient. It proves impossible to be around each other without thinking about their past. Especially when Jessie has been keeping secrets for all this time.

And that's all I'm going to tell you. You'll have to read the book to find out how they move on from those circumstances that forced them apart and watch as that passion flares back to life.

I hope you enjoy their story!

Karin xx

FALLING AGAIN FOR THE SURGEON

KARIN BAINE

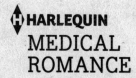

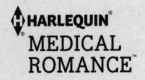

HARLEQUIN®
MEDICAL ROMANCE™

Recycling programs
for this product may
not exist in your area.

ISBN-13: 978-1-335-73783-0

Falling Again for the Surgeon

Harlequin Enterprises ULC
22 Adelaide St. West, 41st Floor
Toronto, Ontario M5H 4E3, Canada
www.Harlequin.com

Printed in U.S.A.

Karin Baine lives in Northern Ireland with her husband, two sons and her out-of-control notebook collection. Her mother and her grandmother's vast collection of books inspired her love of reading and her dream of becoming a Harlequin author. Now she can tell people she has a *proper* job! You can follow Karin on Twitter, @karinbaine1, or visit her website for the latest news—karinbaine.com.

For Stella, Sam & Miriam xx

**Praise for
Karin Baine**

"Emotionally enchanting! The story was fast-paced,
emotionally charged and oh so satisfying!"
—*Goodreads* on *Their One-Night Twin Surprise*

CHAPTER ONE

'I'M NOT HIS MOTHER,' Jessie found herself repeating to the latest attending doctor, as she had to every other medical colleague she'd encountered earlier, on the way through the emergency department with the small child on the stretcher.

'What's his name?' the doctor asked, ignoring her protestations and continuing his examination of the boy's X-rays and CT scans.

She heaved out a sigh of frustration. 'Simon. I don't know his surname or anything else about him. I was simply there when the accident happened. The fire and rescue service are still on scene, trying to get his parents out of the car. He was catapulted through the window into the road. I was in the car behind—I was able to keep him talking for a while until he lost consciousness.' The paramedics had passed on their preliminary findings to the A&E staff but Jessie repeated it, trying to process what she'd witnessed. He'd been in a lot of pain and they'd suspected a spinal cord injury, which was why they'd ordered a battery of tests on his arrival.

'You shouldn't be in here if you're not family.' He attempted to dismiss her but Jessie was reluctant to leave the boy alone when she'd seen how frightened he'd been. She'd stayed with him while he'd been examined and before they'd wheeled him in to X-ray. There should be at least one semi-familiar face when he woke up.

'No, but he was responding to me, and I do work at the hospital.' That info, along with the lanyard she flashed at him, at least made him pause for a second.

'You're a doctor?'

Jessie grimaced. Skating around the facts had got her this far with the busy paramedics but now she'd been rumbled. 'Not exactly. I'm a physiotherapist.'

As expected, that information drew an

eyeroll in response. 'Thank you, Ms… Rea, but I think we can manage without you from here.'

'She can stay for now,' a voice announced as another doctor arrived with a swish of the cubicle curtain.

Jessie was about to thank the new arrival for his compassion when she saw who'd entered, and suddenly lost the power of speech.

'Good to see you, Jessie, though I wish it were in better circumstances.'

Taller than she remembered, his hair a deeper auburn than the red she recalled blazing in the summer sun the last time she'd seen him, Cameron Holmes was as handsome as ever.

'He's not my son,' she blurted, the shock of seeing him again as great as the emergency situation she'd been drawn into on her way home from work.

He paused his glance over his patient's chart to shoot her a smile. 'I gathered that. You can sit with him for now but he'll be going for surgery soon.'

'Surgery?' she repeated, blinking at the vision before her of her first love—the only man she'd ever loved—standing before her. Cameron wasn't so much the one that got away as the one she'd chucked back in the lake in an attempt to give him a second chance at life.

'Yes. The sooner he has surgery, the greater chance there is of him making a full recovery. I'm an orthopaedic surgeon. I specialise in spinal injuries, that's why they called me in. Usually I work in the Belfast Community Hospital.' That explained his somewhat casual attire of paint-splattered jeans and ragged T-shirt along with his sudden appearance at her place of work. If he was on call to cover the area he would've had to drop whatever he was doing and come straight here to the hospital in Innisheg village. She hadn't known he was still living in the country, never mind living less than an hour away from her.

The other attending medics seemed grateful to hand over Simon's care in the meantime so they could go and treat other patients waiting for their attention, leaving Jessie and Cameron alone in the cubicle with the boy.

He must have seen her assessment of his

attire, following her gaze to the large hole at the seam of his tight black crew neck, exposing a tantalising patch of smooth taut skin. 'I was decorating. I'm not usually this unkempt but I didn't want to waste time when every second counts in cases like this.'

It was on the tip of her tongue to tell him he looked good to her when she realised how inappropriate it would seem, not only due to the current circumstances but also because they hadn't parted on the best of terms and hadn't seen each other in nearly fifteen years. She should be more impressed by his career status than how well he'd aged.

'I'm still trying to get my head around the fact that you're a surgeon. All of your hard work really paid off. Your family must be so proud.' It had been his dream to work in medicine, something which had seemed so far out of reach for someone who'd struggled with dyslexia. With hard work and the right support, he'd obviously shown everyone exactly what he was capable of.

Jessie had never doubted him. When she'd studied with him he'd been driven, his work ethic second to none. That was part of the reason she'd fallen for him. Despite the obstacles, how many people had disparaged him, he hadn't let that get in the way of his goal. It was a pity fate had prevented her from following her dreams too.

He raised an eyebrow at her. 'What do you think?'

It was a bucket of cold water over her initial enthusiasm at seeing him in his dream job to find his family were still treating him as abysmally as they always had. She wondered if that was why she hadn't seen him around their hometown since the day he'd left for medical school. Every Christmas or bank holiday weekend she'd wondered if she might run into him, but the dates always came and went without a single sighting. Now she knew why. He'd had nothing to come back for.

'I'm sorry. I thought perhaps, with time, they might have supported you better. You always deserved more. It shouldn't have mattered that you were the youngest of six siblings, they still should have taken care of you.'

'Yes, well, having parents who call you

stupid even after it's discovered you have dyslexia teaches you not to have high expectations. Everything I achieved is down to you and to the support I finally received in high school.'

'I was merely your study buddy. It was you who put in the work. I'm not sure I can take any credit.' Especially when he'd completed his studies in a different part of the country, away from her.

'We both know you were a lot more than that.' He didn't have to say any more than that to stop her arguing, bringing back memories of their time together as teenagers. Before the heartache.

With Cameron's neglectful family and Jessie a young carer for her mother, they'd both been set apart from their classmates, loners who'd gravitated towards each other.

'It didn't take a lot of research to find out that visual stimulation helps dyslexics to retain information and having a good study schedule helped both of us.' She deliberately chose to ignore the reference to their past relationship. It wouldn't do either of them any good to revisit that. Especially when she'd worked so hard to make sure he moved on without her.

He took a moment before he responded, as though he'd toyed with the idea of saying more on the subject then changed his mind.

'I see you went into an area of medicine after all.' He pointed at her work pass, though she was sure he'd already heard what field she'd gone into.

'Yes, physiotherapy meant I could study at the local college instead of the city.'

It was a touchy subject when they'd planned to go to medical school together. The time she'd spent with Cameron had been the happiest of her life, but circumstances had brought that to a swift end.

'Listen, Jessie, I have to go and prep for surgery. It was nice to see you again.' His abrupt exit would suggest he looked back on their time together with less yearning than she did, but she had only herself to blame. She'd broken his heart and now, spying the wedding ring on his finger, she was breaking her own all over again too.

Cameron Holmes was a reminder of everything she'd lost, everything she could never have again. Worse than that, she suspected she was going to see even more of him in the future. As Simon's surgeon he would be overseeing his progress and Jessie would be tasked with helping the boy walk again. And she cared too much to abandon the child simply because of her own discomfort around her childhood sweetheart.

Although she was probably nothing but a footnote in Cameron's story now he appeared to be a successful married surgeon, her highlights reel had begun and ended with him. He was the only man she'd ever loved, ever dared to plan a future with. Now it seemed she was going to have to pay the price for her mistakes by seeing him on a regular basis.

Cameron had to take a moment outside the emergency department to compose himself. Being on call was always full of tension, not knowing what he'd be walking into when he came through the hospital doors. Emergencies he could deal with—his job was fraught with life-changing decisions and surgeries he was ultimately responsible for—but seeing Jessie again was something which had thrown him completely out of his comfort zone.

He clutched his hand to his chest, almost certain he could still feel that hole she'd torn in his heart when she'd dumped him before medical school. It would be much easier if he didn't remember, or if that pain had lessened over time, but neither had happened. He'd simply had to grow around the void she'd left inside him. It had always been there but now it had awakened like an angry volcano, Jessie's reappearance filling him full of anger and hurt. Except there was no room in his life to deal with it all now.

He had enough to keep him occupied, with Thomas and work. Spending time looking back wasn't going to do him any favours now. Especially wondering why he hadn't been enough for her, and if she'd met someone who could give her everything he'd apparently been lacking.

But it wouldn't do anyone any good for him to start soul-searching now. Fifteen years apart was a long time. They were adults who'd gone on to have lives apart from one another, even though there'd been a time when he'd thought he wouldn't survive without her.

Jessie had been the first person who'd ever shown him love and kindness. Perhaps that was what had kept her alive in his heart for so long. He'd put her on a pedestal that not even his wife had been able to reach. Whatever it was about seeing her again that got under his skin, he hoped it was short-lived. Along with their reacquaintance.

He was here to do a job and he'd do it much better without his brown-haired, green-eyed first love monopolising his thoughts.

'Hey, Mum, I'm going to be late tonight so don't wait up for me. There was an accident on the way home. I'm fine, but there was a young boy hurt so I'm staying with him for a while.' While she was waiting for Simon to come out of surgery Jessie phoned home so her mother wouldn't be sitting up worrying about what was keeping her.

Jessie's father had left before she'd been born and her mother had suffered a blood clot during her pregnancy, which had subsequently caused a stroke and left her partially paralysed.

Ever since then Jessie had been burdened with the guilt of thinking she was to blame for her mother's physical decline and she'd spent her life in penance, trying to make up for it. As a result, she still lived at home, taking care of her mother when she wasn't at work.

'Oh, Jessie. Are you sure you're all right?'

'I'm fine. I came along after the accident but this boy's parents were hurt. I thought someone should stay with him until his family can get here.'

'Of course. Is he going to be okay?'

'He had some spinal damage and he's in surgery at the minute.' She hesitated before telling her the rest, unsure if she should mention Cameron when that period of their lives had been a difficult time for both of them. In the end she knew she had to confide in someone when her emotions were in such turmoil and her mother was the only one who could possibly understand.

'Mum, the surgeon is Cameron Holmes,'

she finally said, and it seemed an age before her mother responded.

'Did you tell him?'

Jessie sighed. They'd had this conversation fifteen years ago, before he'd left for medical school, and they still had differing views on the subject. 'No. It wasn't the time or the place.'

'Jessie, he had a right to know then, and he has a right to know now. It would give you both some closure to finally tell him what happened. I know you never got over it, or him, and you've been pushing people away ever since.'

'I don't want to get into this right now, Mum. You know why I didn't tell him what happened. We were eighteen, we weren't ready for a baby, and I didn't want to ruin his future. He would have insisted on dropping out of medical school to take care of us and it didn't seem fair on him to keep him trapped here after he'd worked so hard.'

Even the mention of their baby was enough to make her feel as though her insides were being squeezed until she could barely breathe. She'd been young and foolish, and so carried away with the passion and love she felt for Cameron she'd taken stupid risks. The result being an unplanned pregnancy that threatened both of their futures. She hadn't wanted to lose Cameron but she didn't want to be responsible for ruining someone else's life when she was still burdened with guilt over her mother's ill health. Cameron, being the man he was, would have insisted on staying if he'd known there was a baby on the way, so she hadn't told him, instead simply insisting it was over and that she didn't want to be with him any more. What might have seemed cruel at the time was actually an act of love, setting him free instead of holding him back, the way his own family had done. Though he would never know it.

'You had plenty of time to tell him after you lost the baby. I'm sure Cameron would have understood why you acted the way you did. You could have tried to make a go of things.' Her mother's voice was soft, touching gently on the subject Jessie never wanted to talk about.

The miscarriage had felt like a double loss, as though she was losing Cameron all over again. The one consolation she'd had after their break-up was the knowledge she was carrying a part of him with her. She'd imagined raising a mini-Cameron, all red hair and long legs, pouring all of her love into their son when she couldn't be with his father. To lose the baby so soon after the love of her life had caused her such physical and emotional pain she'd thought she wouldn't survive it. It was as though she'd lost her breath and hadn't been able to catch it again.

If not for her mother's support, Jessie wasn't sure she'd have made it through her grief. Since then she'd put all of her energy into work and looking after her mother so she didn't have time to wallow, mourning everything she'd lost fifteen years ago.

'No, I couldn't. What sort of future would we have had if I couldn't give him children?' It was ironically cruel that the pregnancy she'd been afraid to tell him about had ended in her finding out she had the same health issues as her mother. Antiphospholipid syndrome, a disorder of the immune system, meant she was at great risk of developing blood clots. It also meant a higher risk of miscarriage, and although she now regularly took a small dose of aspirin to thin her blood there were no guarantees she wouldn't miscarry again.

When she and Cameron had talked about their future together he'd made it clear that he wanted a family some day, but only when he had a successful career with the money and time to devote himself to his children. His own upbringing, where he was neglected by his parents, had left a lasting impact on him and he didn't want to inflict that on another generation.

Perhaps if they'd still been together they could've weathered it all, looked into alternatives like adoption, but there wouldn't have been anything to gain by telling him she'd lost his baby and could never give him another one. It had been best to let him live his life and find happiness with someone who could give him a family.

'I still think you should have let him make that decision.'

She could almost see her mother shrugging her shoulders.

'It's in the past, Mum. There's no point

in dragging it up again. He's married, probably with a family. He's moved on. Maybe that's all I need to know so I can do the same.' There'd been many reasons why none of her relationships had worked out over the years—the time she spent looking after her mother, the knowledge that she probably wouldn't have children—but at the heart of it she knew it was because she'd never loved anyone the way she'd loved Cameron.

Now she'd seen for herself the same wasn't true for him, perhaps she could stop comparing everyone else to her first and only love.

'I'm sure you know best.' Her mother's tone, sounding much like the one she'd used when Jessie had sent him off to medical school without telling him about the baby, suggested different.

'I didn't phone to discuss the past and the what-might-have-beens. I just wanted you to know I'll be late home tonight.' Jessie put an end to the subject, refusing to venture down that road when she'd spent too long wondering if she'd made the right decision at the time. Now she knew he was a successful married surgeon, it appeared she had. All she had to do was reconcile herself with the past and her own actions and maybe she'd find someone else too.

'Okay. I'll say a prayer for you all before I go to sleep. 'Night, Jessie.'

''Night, Mum.' Jessie ended the call, her burden a little lighter after sharing the evening's events with the only other person who knew the real history she had with Cameron.

It was going to be a long night, not only waiting for news on Simon's surgery but also because she'd likely spend the time revisiting the past in her head. Seeing Cameron again was making her confront the decisions she'd made and she was afraid that, under such scrutiny, she might realise that not all of them had been for the best.

CHAPTER TWO

'IT'S NEVER EASY when it's a child,' Bobby, the anaesthetist, commented as they waited for the anaesthetic to kick in.

'No. I mean, surgery is never routine when you have someone's life in your hands, but one mistake or complication and this is a child that might never walk again.' Cameron was performing spinal fusion surgery to join the damaged vertebrae the boy had sustained in the accident, to provide stability and relieve pressure on the spinal cord. If left untreated there could be permanent damage but, hopefully, operating so soon after the accident would preserve a healthy blood flow to the spinal cord after the trauma suffered.

'No pressure then.'

He could see the smile in Bobby's eyes,

even though his mouth was hidden behind his surgical mask. Although they were a team in the operating theatre, Cameron took personal responsibility for his patients. Simon, who couldn't be much younger than his own son, Thomas, had his whole life in front of him if he did his job well.

He thought of his ten-year-old son and the lengths he'd gone to so he could lead a normal life. Although it had likely caused the breakdown of his marriage, he'd fought until they'd got Thomas's ADHD diagnosis so they could give him the support he needed. Ciara hadn't understood his fixation on giving their son 'a label', nor had she been able to cope with their son's extra needs. But Cameron had been there and knew how important it was to get Thomas the right help in order for him to have all the same opportunities available to his peers. He was determined to do the same for Simon with this operation.

Once they were satisfied that Simon was completely under the anaesthetic, Cameron made the first incision along his back. The procedure meant painstakingly removing debris from the injury site so he could then pack bone in and around the metal screws needed for extra support, and to promote further healing in the damaged vertebrae.

'Clamps, please.'

It was a surgery he'd undertaken many times before but he was feeling under more pressure than usual, having seen Jessie Rea again, and by the time he'd finished stabilising the damaged bone, sweat was forming on his brow.

Both he and Jessie wanted this boy to recover from his ordeal and he knew her kind heart would deny her the chance to walk away. She was a physiotherapist, exactly who Simon would need to help him back to full mobility. It was guaranteed she would be first in line to offer the boy her professional assistance and with a shared patient they were fated to work together—the very sort of distraction he did not need in his life.

He closed up the vertical incision he'd made at the injury site, knowing he'd done everything in his power to prevent this from being a life-changing injury. As long as there were no unforeseen complications,

Simon would be able to start his rehabilitation and get back to some semblance of normality. The same might not be said for him now Jessie was back on the scene.

He'd never believed the spiel she'd given him at the time of their split because of the love they'd shared, the plans they'd made. Jessie was not the kind of cold-hearted woman to walk away from anyone without a good explanation. Yet he'd let her, figuring if she really didn't want to be with him there was no point sticking around to debate the matter. He'd wanted to get away from his family and he'd believed the same to be true about Jessie with her mother. So he'd gone on without her, never looking back because it was too painful. Jessie had become just another person to disregard his feelings, to cast him aside as though he were nothing and remind him he was unworthy of love.

Before he'd had the opportunity to change out of his scrubs he was seeking her out. He found her in the canteen. It had long since stopped serving hot food but it was well lit, comfortable and kitted out with vending machines packed with snacks and hot drinks.

He hadn't planned to stay any longer than it took to give her an update on Simon's progress but the sight of tears streaking down her face was sufficient to make him pull up a chair at her table. 'What's wrong? What happened?'

'Simon's parents didn't make it. That poor boy.' She burst into loud hiccupping sobs, prompting Cameron to take her hands in his.

'I'm so sorry, Jessie.' Offering condolences to anyone else in this situation might have seemed absurd. By all accounts she didn't know anything about the family beyond witnessing what had befallen them tonight. But, unless she'd changed dramatically in the fifteen years since he'd seen her, he knew Jessie would take the news badly. She cared as deeply and completely for strangers as she did for loved ones.

It was the very reason he'd fallen for her in the first place and the reason he found it difficult to reconcile this version of her with the Jessie who'd coldly told him she no longer wanted a future with him.

'I am sorry to hear about young Simon's

parents.' Cameron directed the conversation back to the reason they were both here.

'How did his surgery go? Will he recover?'

'It went as well as could be expected. I don't foresee any problems with his recovery, at least nothing physical.'

'I know, the poor mite. Social services will have to get involved now to try and find family willing to take him in.' Her heart broke for the child whose life had changed in an instant. His future was uncertain and now he would have to learn to walk all over again. It was a lot for someone of that age to face all at once.

'I know I'm being ridiculous.' She sniffed. 'I don't know the family at all but I can't help feeling sorry for poor Simon.'

She lapsed back into tears, her compassion manifesting in liquid form.

'Hey, you've been through a lot tonight too. It's only natural for you to be emotional. Have you had a check-up yourself?' Shock after a traumatic event like a crash was real and, though not physically injured, Jessie had nonetheless experienced emotional trauma. Processing what had happened, including the deaths of people involved, could have a definite impact on her mental health.

'I'll be fine. I'm not the one who was hurt.' She pulled her hand away from his to wipe her eyes. She was the same Jessie who had always put everyone else's needs before her own. Not for the first time he wondered if she'd had a more altruistic motive for ending their relationship. He had no clue what that could have been but it made more sense that she'd been trying to protect him from something rather than suddenly deciding a life together was something she no longer wanted.

'You should go home and rest. Do you have someone who could come and get you, and look after you?' It was likely she would suffer flashbacks and a sleepless night replaying the horrific details of the car accident. She should have someone to comfort her, to support her in her time of need, the way she had done for him when they were younger.

Cameron was no longer part of her life, or someone she cared for, and he found he was envious of the man who got to do that for her. To hold her in his arms and kiss her was a privilege not to be taken for granted, as he'd learned too late.

'No, I… There's only Mum.'

'You're still living at home? What about all those plans you had to travel?' That was the main excuse she'd given to end their best-laid plans. A sudden need for space so she could explore the big wide world instead of being trapped in a relationship at too young an age.

What a kick in the teeth it was to find she had stayed and never spread her wings. It was a disservice to both of them that she hadn't gone on some epic soul-searching, life-changing adventure after all.

'I never left.' Jessie hung her head, knowing her mother was right. He did deserve to know and have some closure on that shock break-up she'd sprung on him.

'Why do I think there's more about that time that I don't know?'

'Because there is.'

'Okay…' He folded his arms and waited

for her to fill in the blanks in their history, a task both daunting and long overdue, yet she knew they wouldn't be able to move on if she wasn't completely honest with him.

She was also aware it wasn't going to be easy, either for her to say or for Cameron to hear.

'I was never going to go travelling.'

'Apparently not, but why did you feel you had to lie to me, Jessie? If you didn't want to be with me you could have just been honest with me.' There was tension already in his voice, anger and frustration at her lies building in him. If he was ticked off now she couldn't imagine how he'd react when he heard the full story.

Jessie gulped, hoping that his past feelings for her meant that eventually he would forgive her.

'I wanted to be with you more than anything but—'

Cameron opened his mouth as though he was about to interrupt her, but she had to get this all out now.

'I was pregnant.'

'What?' He seemed to slump in his chair,

that apparent rage extinguished by his shock. Jessie could not have felt more guilty about being responsible for that look of anguish on his face.

'I didn't want to stop you achieving your dream of being a doctor because of one stupid mistake. I thought by telling you a white lie, by ending things between us, you would move on and forget about me.'

'You were wrong.'

'Was I? You're married, I'm not.' It was a low blow considering that was her motivation to act the way she had. The whole idea had been for him to move on and live his life, yet the fact he had done so without her still ate away at her. Because they should have been together, raising their child.

'What was I supposed to do, Jessie? You told me you didn't want to be with me. I believed it. Should I have spent the last fifteen years alone, mourning the loss of our relationship? The one you told me you didn't want?'

She couldn't answer when that was exactly what she had done.

* * *

'If I'd known there was a baby involved I would have stayed and looked after you both.' Cameron's head was buzzing with memories of that time, of how things could have been so different. It felt like a betrayal for Jessie to have lied to him about how she felt, making decisions about his life without even consulting him. She'd broken his heart for no reason when he would easily have chosen her and their baby over his career. He would have made it work if it meant being with her and having a family of his own.

'That's exactly why I didn't tell you. You'd worked so hard—I didn't want to be the one to take that away from you.'

'Yet you took everything else away from me. The chance to be part of the decision-making or to have a family with you. I would have chosen you, Jessie. Every single time.' Despite the urge to shout and scream over the injustice of it all, his voice was barely more than a whisper, so filled with emotion it was beginning to crack. It didn't help seeing tears glistening in Jessie's eyes at his reaction.

She'd denied him this information for fifteen years. They could've had a teenager by now, saved two people from an unhappy marriage. He wasn't sure he could ever forgive her for keeping such a huge, life-altering secret.

'I just wanted you to be happy,' she said, reaching out for him.

He shrugged her hand off his arm, unable to bear her touch when he was struggling to process what she'd done to him. 'Yeah? How's that going for you?'

'I'm sorry, Cameron. I know I should've been honest with you at the time but I thought it was for the best. No one in your life had ever put you first and I thought I was doing the right thing for you.'

'How admirable.' He knew he was being facetious but he couldn't see past his own pain at present. No, he couldn't remember the last time anyone had done that for him but he wasn't convinced it had been the right call for either of them.

It shouldn't surprise him that Jessie had carried it all on her shoulders when she'd always been mature beyond her years, taking on more responsibility than any young girl should ever have endured on her own because of her situation at home. But it didn't make it the right decision. It said a lot about their relationship then if she'd felt she couldn't talk to him about such an important subject, just as Ciara had been unable to discuss her feelings with him during their marriage. Perhaps he'd been the problem, not approachable or compassionate enough for the women in his life to feel safe including him in huge decisions affecting their lives.

'Was I really so unapproachable?'

'Not at all. Please don't think that. I guess I was simply trying to protect you. You'd been through so much at home and at school, I didn't want to give you more problems.'

It went some way to easing his conscience to find out he hadn't been some sort of monster to his exes but it didn't ease the hurt of not knowing the full circumstances of their break-up until now. When it was too late to do anything about it.

'And the baby? Why didn't you tell me about it later on?' He swallowed down the sudden swell of nausea accompanying the thought of what had happened. If she'd got rid of their baby, or had it adopted, without his say in the matter, it would be a betrayal he could never come back from. The child had two parents, even if one of them hadn't known about its existence.

He could see the pain surrounding that time there on her face even before she spoke.

'I had a miscarriage before the end of my first trimester. I didn't even get to see it on a scan.'

'I'm sorry. I wish I could have been there for you both. I wish you would have let me.' Learning about the baby they might have had together, then finding out it had died, was too much to take in in the space of one short conversation. It changed their whole history, the life he should have had. With Jessie. They should have mourned their baby together but she'd done it alone. As he would now have to do.

'I'm sorry, Cameron. There didn't seem any point in upsetting you...' Her voice trailed off, as though she knew it was a lame excuse.

The whole time he'd been studying and

beginning his new independent life, Jessie had been left behind, dealing with the aftermath of their relationship—a pregnancy and a loss. He hadn't been there to console her or say goodbye to their baby. Though that wasn't his fault, it would stay with him for ever.

'I… I gotta go, Jessie.'

'Are we okay? I mean, I know this was a lot to drop on you.'

'I just need some time.'

'Of course.'

He heard the disappointment and regret in her voice but he needed to focus on his own feelings right now and work through them before he could even look at Jessie again.

'I'll liaise with social services every step of the way where Simon is concerned. It's important if anyone does come forward that they know exactly what they're dealing with. It won't be easy to take on a grieving child, and one who's suffered a debilitating injury at that. I can't do anything to improve his family circumstances, but I will be there to provide any advice or assistance required for his recovery.' He was clearly setting boundaries between them. It was no wonder that he wanted some distance after everything she'd hit him with tonight, but she would have preferred it if he'd stay to talk through his feelings.

Although that was something he'd never been particularly good at. She'd always had to guess what was bothering him and gradually coax the information out of him. That was likely due to his upbringing when his family had never validated his feelings, or even acknowledged them. Still, he was an adult now and she would have thought if he was married he would've learned how to communicate better.

The idea that he might be going home to discuss the intimate details of their personal relationship with his wife made her stomach lurch. She'd kept their baby to herself for all this time and it seemed a betrayal for him to share it with another woman, even though he hadn't been hers in a long time.

'You're staying on?' That information eventually penetrated through the fog of grief to reach her brain.

It was one thing running into Cameron unexpectedly, dealing with the feelings suddenly thrust forward in the highly emotive circumstances. However, it would be entirely different if she were to be working alongside him on a more regular basis.

'I would like to continue monitoring my patient's progress, yes. Why, would you have a problem with that?' Cameron held her gaze, challenging her to be brave and admit it would be difficult for her to be reminded every day of the love she'd thrown away.

It crossed her mind to do so, but she was already too invested in Simon to simply walk away and leave him.

'No. Not at all. We've both moved on and the past should stay there. It's Simon's needs that matter. I'm sure we can work together to give him the best possible chance of recovery without our personal history getting in the way.'

Jessie rose from her chair and on slightly unsteady legs tossed her empty cup into the bin as she made her exit.

She wasn't sure if she imagined the voice behind her saying, 'Let's hope so.'

CHAPTER THREE

'Now, Simon, you know we have to do these exercises to keep your muscles working.' Jessie attempted again to pull back the covers on the hospital bed in order to start his physiotherapy.

They had established a few things in the few days since he'd had his surgery—Simon was seven years old, his surname was Armstrong, he didn't have any siblings or other immediate family, and he was stubborn as a mule when he wanted to be.

'Go away,' Simon cried, bunching the sheet tighter in his fists.

'That's not very nice, Simon. Ms Rea is only trying to help you.' Trust Cameron to walk in when their patient was being combative and making her look incompetent. Yesterday Simon had been as meek as a lamb, complying with her every instruction, but, as all young children, his mood was as changeable as the weather.

The boy huffed out a breath and relinquished his hold of the bedcovers on the doctor's command. She'd almost have preferred Simon to maintain his resistance and see Cameron sweat for a bit. They had to make allowances for the boy's age and circumstances, but on days like this it didn't make dealing with him any less problematic. Especially when the prospect of Cameron popping up like this at any time added to the pressure. Any attempt to portray herself as the capable, independent woman she wanted him to see her as was thwarted in the opposition of her patient. It was important Cameron should see her in a positive light to make her sacrifice seem worthwhile, even if the truth differed.

He would probably never forgive her for what she'd done when he'd been so distant around her since she'd told him about the baby. It wasn't surprising, she supposed, but it was hard when they used to be so close.

All she could do was get on with her job

and try to make a positive difference in her patients' lives. Even if she'd messed up her own.

'I know the exercises aren't fun for you, Simon, but I promise they will help you get better.'

He relented with a huff and with no further resistance she was able to peel away the sheet and begin to manipulate his limbs. Getting him mobile again as soon as possible was important but he was still in pain after the surgery. For now it would be one less hurdle to get over if she maintained the strength in those limbs in the meantime. It was necessary to keep the muscles and joints moving so they didn't atrophy.

'I'm bored. When can I play football?'

Jessie glanced at Cameron for guidance on the matter. It was he who would have the final say on their patient's capabilities. When Simon was ready Jessie would take over his recovery, working to get him back to full strength in terms of his mobility.

Cameron perched on the side of the bed and faced Simon directly. 'Do you remember how we talked about how sometimes we have to do something we don't really like before we get to do the good stuff?'

'Like having to eat broccoli before I can have my jelly and ice cream?'

'Exactly.' Cameron ruffled his hair affectionately. They seemed to have formed quite a bond and Jessie didn't think it was merely because he was Cameron's patient. He was a father, he knew how to talk to and interact with a young boy. More than that, he cared. Cameron had taken it upon himself to break the news about his parents, once they'd established a rapport and got social services' approval. Jessie, as a familiar face in the absence of any family members to be found, had been in attendance for the heart-wrenching moment. Cameron had been compassionate and sympathetic, holding the boy tightly in his arms while he sobbed. He'd offered the love and support she doubted he'd had himself growing up. She imagined the relationship he would have had with their child and it made her yearn even more for the family she would never have.

Social services were doing their best to place Simon with family and keep track of his progress, but with their other caseloads to keep track of, and different care workers visiting, they hadn't completely gained his trust. He often grew upset at the notion that they were going to take him away, not an unjustified fear, given the circumstances, but their involvement wasn't helping aid his recovery.

She and Cameron were his only constants at present and sometimes it felt as though they were a little dysfunctional family of their own. They'd assumed the interim role as his guardians, coaxing him to heed their instructions for his own benefit, taking turns playing good cop and bad cop, and whatever else it took to get him back on his feet.

Jessie let herself indulge in a moment of folly, daydreaming of just such a scenario. If she'd told him about the pregnancy, if she'd been able to carry to full term, they might've had a family of their own and enjoyed a love she'd failed to find with any other.

But, given the chance to do things over, she knew even now, if their baby had lived, she still would have chosen Cameron's future happiness over her own. It was a futile exercise anyway, looking back and wondering what if, knowing she would never get to experience the joy of having a husband or family, the things most people took for granted.

'Jessie and I are working together to get you back on your feet as soon as possible, but if we rush things it might exacerbate your injury.'

'That would mean it takes longer for you to heal and have more physiotherapy. Extra stretches,' she added, bending and straightening Simon's legs, flexing them to keep him supple.

'Yuck!' He rolled his eyes.

'Exactly, so be patient,' she reminded him as she finished rubbing down his legs with soothing lotion.

'I could do with some of that myself,' Cameron said, stretching out his back as he stood up.

Jessie arched an eyebrow at him.

'I mean a massage in general. I'm getting old. Some of us have to pay for that sort of thing.'

She couldn't help but snort as he dug

himself deeper into a hole. He flashed her a scowl, suggesting her laughter wasn't appropriate, but she was enjoying seeing him on the back foot for once. It was nice to know Cameron was human and he was capable of making a fool of himself too.

In the old days he would have laughed at himself but after opening up old wounds and rubbing salt in them with the news about their baby he'd been cool towards her. It made her almost want to volunteer to help him with whatever ailed him, to try and mend some bridges. However, she managed to catch herself in time, knowing that having her hands on his body was never going to help her get over him. He was still an attractive man and her memories and vivid imagination wouldn't do anything to help her move on if he was stripped to the waist for her.

Thankfully he made to leave so she didn't feel obliged to offer her healing services after all.

'I have to go, Simon, but make sure you do everything Jessie tells you. I'll see you both again in the morning.'

'Okay.' Simon gave Cameron a fist bump, followed by some convoluted handshake they'd made up as though they were members of some secret society she wasn't party to.

'I'll walk out with you. Simon, get some rest for now, but make sure you practise those exercises I gave you before I see you tomorrow.'

'Okay.' Simon sounded miserable.

He obviously didn't anticipate her next visit with as much excitement as Dr Holmes', but she didn't take it personally as they left the ward. She was just glad Simon was responding so well after his surgery. Some children might have shut down completely after the trauma of the crash and losing two parents but, even though he was a bit resistant to his physical rehabilitation, the presence of that feisty spirit was a good sign. He would need it to get him through this ordeal.

Cameron was flicking through his notes as they walked down the corridor, paying little attention to Jessie. It would be difficult to tell they'd ever been in a relationship, had talked about living together and getting married one day, when he treated her like every other member of staff. He was courteous and co-operative but didn't go beyond a respectful professional discourse with her.

Whereas over the course of the last few days she'd been increasingly curious about the life and times of Dr Cameron Holmes, keen to find out if he was the same man she'd known way back before she'd broken both of their hearts. He didn't give much away, seemingly more guarded and private than the quiet teen she'd befriended and fallen in love with.

Extra guilt piled onto her shoulders at the thought that she'd caused him to increase his defences. But, then again, perhaps this armour he wore was something he donned only when in contact with her, reserved for someone who'd let him down more than once.

Jessie was determined not to do it again.

Someone let the double doors on a side ward swing behind them, causing a gust of air to catch Cameron's notes out of his hands. The pages blew halfway down the corridor, falling at different intervals like drifting autumn leaves.

'Let me help you get those.' Jessie began snatching up the escaped notes, trying to make amends with every small gesture she could manage.

'I've got it,' he insisted, a muscle in his jaw twitching with irritation. It wasn't that he was rude to her, but she still knew him well enough to see he was ill at ease around her. Despite the life he'd gone on to have without her, he clearly hadn't forgiven her for the way they'd parted. And now he'd been apprised of the reasons she'd done so his behaviour was justified. For Jessie, it was too late for recriminations and regret. She'd done all that a long time ago.

The past was the past and it was clear he wanted it to stay there.

He gathered the pages and hurried on without looking back. Just as he'd apparently done fifteen years ago.

Cameron knew he'd have to stop spending so much time with Jessie. Of course he was overseeing Simon's recovery but the visits during his physiotherapy sessions were proving challenging. It had been clear since their unexpected reunion that there was going to be a problem. They had unfinished business and his feelings for her had sprung back to life the moment he'd set eyes on her again.

Yet nothing could have prepared him for what she'd told him. A baby. It was difficult to come to terms with the idea that she'd been carrying his child at that time, when she'd told him she no longer wanted to be with him. Everything could have been so different and it was difficult to forgive her for keeping it all from him, even the miscarriage. They should have grieved the loss together.

His emotions were complicated and fragile like a gossamer web. It would be easier if he only thought badly of her, but at the same time he was still attracted to her and the person she was now. Time hadn't made her any less compassionate or patient—the qualities which had made him fall for her in the first place. He was doing his best not to think that way, but it was proving to be a task beyond his capabilities.

Never mind that he hadn't been with a woman at all in the years since Ciara left.

This was Jessie, the woman he'd never stopped loving. It wasn't easy to simply forget someone he'd thought he'd be with for ever.

He also had questions that he wasn't sure he wanted to know the answers to. Did she have a husband and family of her own? Why hadn't she loved him enough?

But he wouldn't ask. He shouldn't care and he'd been hurt too much by those he'd loved to add to those scars.

As soon as Simon was able to be discharged Cameron would sever all ties to Jessie and go back to the life he'd been leading without her. Until then he'd do his best to remain level-headed and focus on his patient, not his personal issues.

Although he was a few feet ahead of her, trying not to engage, he could hear her quick steps trying to catch up with him. It was only when he was faced with the sight of his tearful son and the childminder that he came to a standstill.

'Thomas? What's wrong?' He was accustomed to his son's emotional outbursts but he looked genuinely upset by something and it wasn't like Maggie to bring him to Cameron's place of work. Usually she was able to pacify him until Cameron got home.

When his son didn't answer but continued to weep uncontrollably he looked to the older woman holding him by the hand.

'I'm sorry, Doctor, but he was so upset I was worried he'd hurt himself.'

His red-faced son's wailing was now drawing attention from passing patients and though Cameron tried not to be embarrassed by his son's displays of frustration he was aware it was becoming distressing for those on their way to the children's ward.

Even Jessie had caught up with them now and he knew he'd have to explain what was going on. So far he'd managed to avoid sharing anything of his private life, ashamed at the failure of his marriage, and wanting to protect Thomas. Being divorced reaffirmed the idea that no one loved him enough to stay with him. He didn't want Jessie to pity him or even get close enough to know he had a son, but it was too late now.

'There's an empty office down here if you want some privacy,' Jessie said, immediately making him feel churlish about letting her in on his life when he was aware how sensitive and caring she was with everyone—exactly what he and Thomas needed right now.

'Thanks.' He waited until they were behind closed doors before he made introductions. 'This is my son, Thomas, and Maggie, my childminder.'

'Nice to meet you.' Jessie acknowledged the older woman before she bent down to speak to Thomas. 'And you're the spitting image of your daddy when he was younger. We used to be friends a long time ago and now we work together.'

It seemed so simple when she said it. As though there was nothing for him to be afraid of as his past and present collided in front of his eyes. Though 'friends' or 'colleagues' could never hope to adequately convey the relationship they had back then or now. It was difficult to work alongside someone and not show any emotion. Even though he'd once loved this woman she'd broken his heart and only decided to tell him fifteen years later it had been because she'd been pregnant with, and later lost, his baby. He defied anyone to stay neutral in those circumstances.

Thomas momentarily stopped sobbing to stare at Jessie, wiping the tears away with the back of his hand to leave a grimy smear of dirt on his cheek, seemingly already captivated by her.

'Do you want me to go and give you some privacy?' Jessie asked.

'No. It's fine.' Now that she'd met his son there seemed no point in sending her away, especially when she'd managed to calm Thomas down so that Cameron could find out what had happened.

Cameron pulled over a chair and sat down so he was at eye level with his son, doing his best not to intimidate or frighten him and simply let him explain.

'Teacher…said… I…can't…do…it.' He hiccupped before breaking down into loud messy tears again.

Cameron looked to Maggie for some sort of explanation.

'The class are doing a home project on the subject of their choice. There's a prize for the best one but his teacher thought that, under the circumstances, Thomas might want to sit it out.'

With the suggestion that his son was being prevented from participating in something which was upsetting him to this degree, Cameron's body was already tensing up, preparing for a fight. He'd been doing that almost from the moment Thomas had been born, challenging the system to take care of his son better than they had him.

'Thomas has someone in the classroom to help him with his learning difficulties,' he explained to Jessie. 'Unfortunately, it's not so easy to get the work done at home when I'm working a lot, but we'll figure something out, won't we, buddy?' He gave Thomas a fist bump because a hug wasn't always welcome. Even when he wanted to gather his son up and squeeze him tight, protect him from the outside world.

'I'm sorry, Dr Holmes, but I can't help with his homework either. All this modern technology is beyond me, unfortunately.' Even Maggie was beginning to get upset about the situation, which might have been avoidable if the school had consulted him before dropping this bombshell on Thomas. He knew the teachers were over-stretched and most likely thought they were doing a good thing by excusing Thomas from taking part, but excluding him from activities was exactly what Cameron had fought against.

'I know, Maggie. You're a great help picking Thomas up from school and looking after him until I finish work. This isn't your problem and you did the right thing by bringing him here. I'll have a word with the school and see if we can work something out.'

'He needs a mother. It's not healthy for either of you to be cooped up in that house together all the time.' Maggie, as usual, overstepped the mark in discussing his personal business, but since she was the only help he had in looking after Thomas he couldn't very well disagree with her. It didn't help that she was partly correct. Thomas did need someone in his life, someone who could devote the time and love his mother hadn't managed to give him.

Jessie was watching the exchange, taking everything in, and thanks to Maggie's oversharing he was going to have to admit to the failure of his marriage too.

'His mother left three years ago.' He kept it blunt and to the point. Jessie didn't need to know the painful details, and he certainly didn't want to go into them with an audience which included the son who could barely remember her. It wasn't going to do anything other than embarrass them both and upset Thomas to tell Jessie that Ciara hadn't loved him enough, or that he hadn't considered his wife's feelings as much as his son's. That she hadn't felt as though she could talk to him and tell him she was unhappy, or that he hadn't seen it. Either way, he hadn't been a good husband and it wasn't something he was proud of.

'Oh. I'm sorry.' She already looked uncomfortable with that small snippet of information, glancing back at the closed door, probably preparing her escape from the awkward position she was in.

'It just means we're a little short on baby-sitters. I have another appointment, Maggie.

Can you look after him here until I've finished? I can give you some money to take him to the canteen, or I think there's a play park—'

'I can't stay, Dr Holmes. It will take me another hour to get home on the bus and my granddaughter is coming to stay. I'm sorry.' Maggie was twisting the handle of her bag in her hands, clearly worried about adding to his burden, but Cameron couldn't think badly of her because she had a life and family of her own.

'It's fine, Maggie. You go on home. Thomas can stay with me. Thanks for bringing him over.'

She made sure Thomas had all of his school belongings before she left and Cameron gave her a hug to show there weren't any hard feelings on his part. It wasn't her fault that the school had messed up, that Thomas had had a meltdown, or that he had no one else in his life who could step in to help in a crisis.

'I can take him with me if it would help?' Jessie, who'd been standing quietly since the revelation about his absent wife, stepped forward.

'I'm sure you're busy.' It was one thing seeing her every day and attempting to keep a lid on his emotions, but they'd be moving into dangerous territory if he let her get close to Thomas. He was trying to keep her out of his life, not bring her further into it. If Thomas hadn't been so upset and needing a safe space, she wouldn't even be in here, intruding in his family business.

'I've finished for the day and was just about to head home.'

'But you've got your mother to look after.' If it wasn't for their personal history and his wounded heart he would've jumped at the chance for such help. He probably would have accepted it from anyone other than her, but he was still reeling from the revelation of what she'd done a decade and a half ago. There was no way he wanted a second round, to find out what else she was capable of inflicting upon him.

'Cameron, you need someone to keep an eye on him and I'm volunteering an hour of my time. I can stay here or I can take him

home. If that's okay with you, Thomas?'
She included Thomas in the conversation,
displaying some understanding of what she
was dealing with here. Being in the medical profession, they were both used to dealing with children, often with special needs
requiring that little bit more attention and
sensitivity.

'Here,' Cameron spat out quickly. The
last thing he needed was to set foot back
in his home town, and into Jessie's house,
when he was already struggling to cope
with simply seeing her at work. It would
be too much seeing the people and places
which had hurt him so deeply, not only
crossing that line between their working
and professional relationship but entangling
their lives again, when he should be doing
everything he could to protect himself, and
Thomas, from any further pain. Getting involved, in any capacity, with the woman
who had taken his heart and stomped it ca-
sually into the ground was only ever going
to be trouble. Even if it only destroyed his
peace of mind.

However, the fact that he had no one else to turn to, and that Thomas had stopped crying since Jessie started talking, was the clincher.

'Good. You go and see your patient and Thomas and I will keep ourselves occupied.' She tried to usher him out but Cameron was still reluctant to leave his son, even with a qualified medical professional whom he'd known for a long time.

The original vetting process to find a suitable childminder had been rigorous, but he'd needed someone he could trust completely to deal with Thomas's physical and emotional needs. His son had been through enough upheaval with Ciara abandoning him and the challenges he was facing at school and with his peers. It wouldn't have been fair to inflict a series of unsuitable carers upon him too, and so Cameron was a touch overprotective.

'Just go, Dad.' It was Thomas in the end who finally persuaded him to go, clearly embarrassed by this display from his helicopter parent.

'I'll be back in an hour. Here's my number in case you need me.'

'We'll be fine,' Jessie insisted, but she put his mind at ease by taking it anyway.

CHAPTER FOUR

JESSIE WAS STILL in a state of shock as Cameron left the room, leaving her with his son. His son. It was going to take a while for that to sink in. Looking at Thomas was like glimpsing back in history, and not all of it was to her liking. It was a reminder that Cameron had moved on quite quickly.

Although the end of their relationship had been at her behest, it was a blow to come face to face with the child he'd had with another woman. He hadn't known about their baby, or the loss she'd suffered, until recently, so he wouldn't have understood how meeting Thomas cut her so deep. Perhaps later when he'd had time to think about it he would realise how big a moment it was to her. It was telling, however, that he hadn't mentioned the end of his marriage, or the existence of his son, until he'd been forced to, making it clear he didn't want her to know anything about his personal life.

She probably deserved that. In his eyes she'd abandoned him as much as his wife had, and his family was none of her business. In other circumstances she would have left it at that and backed away, aware that he had no desire to let her anywhere near his son or his life. Except she could see how upset Thomas was and what a bind they'd been left in. Neither of them should get worked up over a spot of babysitting. She was just a colleague doing him a favour. He wouldn't be indebted to her, she wouldn't expect anything from him in return. And once Cameron had finished work and collected Thomas, that would be the end of their association, outside of the workplace. It appeared that neither of them wanted to revisit their past and they were begrudgingly putting up with each other for the sake of their young patient in the children's ward.

For now she simply had to keep Thomas calm and busy enough to take his mind off his school problems until Cameron collected him.

'I don't think there's much for you to do in here. Would you like to come with me to the children's ward and we'll see if we can pick up some games for you to play?' It was really the only child-friendly part of the hospital and they usually kept a cupboard full of toys and books to stimulate the children who were bed-bound due to their health problems. She was sure the ward sister wouldn't mind if she borrowed a few things for a while, but she didn't want to leave Thomas unsupervised and risk Cameron's wrath.

It was clear he was protective of his son and she could understand that when his family had failed to look after him. He was overcompensating for the rough time he'd had growing up, but she knew Thomas would benefit from his father's harrowing experience. His mother and father had shown him how *not* to parent and Jessie knew he would give his own child all the attention and support he'd never had. Especially since his wife was apparently out of the picture too. She might never be party to the details of the break-up but she was sure Cameron loved him enough for two parents.

'Will there be art stuff?' Thomas asked, wiping his nose on his sleeve, his problems temporarily forgotten with the novelty of his new surroundings.

'Sure. Do you like drawing?' If she could find something he was interested in it could make this afternoon easier. They were strangers to one another and she didn't know how Thomas would react to being around her any more than she knew what it would do to her to spend time with Cameron's son. The child they should have had together.

He rummaged in his school backpack and pulled out a sketchpad, foisting it on her without a word.

Dutifully perusing the contents, she braced herself to face the childish scrawls of the average school kid, ready to feign admiration to keep his spirits high. As it turned out, she didn't need to.

'Thomas, these are amazing.' She turned the pages quickly, greedily taking in the pencil-drawn images with splashes of water-colour highlighting the details of the scenes he'd captured.

He shrugged. 'Can we go now?'

'Yes. I'll just send your dad a text so he knows where we are.' He hadn't said she couldn't leave the room with his son but she wanted to keep on the right side of him. She also didn't want him to worry unnecessarily if he came back and found them missing.

Jessie led Thomas to the ward and got permission from the ward sister before bringing him in. Ordinarily she wasn't sure if she would be permitted but mentioning he was a surgeon's son apparently opened doors. Namely the one to the toy cupboard.

She rifled through the stacks of board games and mentally did a fist pump when she found a stack of paper. Her euphoria was short-lived when she realised it was pages of crude outlines for the younger children to colour.

'I suppose we could turn them over and use the back. There must be some paint or pens in here somewhere.' She reached further back but, aside from a few broken chubby crayons, there wasn't much that would pass for art supplies.

'I'll go and ask one of the nurses—' When Jessie turned around to find Thomas was no longer there her heart just about stopped.

She quickly got to her feet, scanning the corridor for her charge, her mouth suddenly dry when she couldn't see him. 'Thomas? Where are you?'

It wasn't in her nature to panic but Cameron had been so concerned about leaving his son in the first place and now he was missing within minutes. The more she looked for him and called his name, the harder her heart pounded. Her concern for Thomas was as great as the worry about how Cameron would kill her for letting him leave her sight for even a second.

'Have you seen Dr Holmes' son? He was here just a second ago.' Jessie went back to the ward sister in case he'd retraced their steps.

'I think he's making friends.' She nodded towards the beds across the hall, sending Jessie running to find him.

'Thomas? What are you doing in here?

You shouldn't have run away like that. What on earth would I have told your father if I hadn't found you?' The relief of seeing him was manifested in her rambling to the bemused ten-year-old who was sitting at Simon's bedside.

'I wanted to paint,' he said, with no indication he understood the distress he'd caused in the short time since he'd left her sight.

'Okay, but I need you to tell me if you want to go somewhere.' Jessie couldn't be too hard on him when she was the one who'd offered to look after him and should have done a better job of it. It was good to see he was not only safe but also providing Simon with some company.

Seeing him sharing the paints and paper with the boy who didn't have anyone else in the world choked her up. Simon was propped up, the table over his bed covered in art supplies, happily drawing away with his new friend sitting beside him.

'Simon, this is Thomas, Dr Holmes' son.' It might be a bit unorthodox to have him in the ward but since they'd already met she thought she should make some introductions. She didn't think Cameron would mind when he was very fond of this particular patient and had become an important male figure in his life.

All the other children on the ward had their parents and other relatives visiting, it would do Simon good to have some company and Thomas seemed to be happy. She pulled up a chair beside him, content to simply watch over him until his father returned.

The three of them sat in companionable silence and Jessie watched as the boys daubed poster paints on sheets of paper. Simon had drawn himself playing football, no doubt something he was desperately wanting to do once he was back on his feet. Thomas had begun painting a woodland scene, outlining the silhouette of a magnificent tree with branches reaching up towards a starry night sky. He really was talented.

'Jessie? What the hell is going on?' Cameron appeared, looking a little flushed.

Even though she hadn't done anything wrong she immediately felt guilty about sitting here with Thomas and Simon. 'Didn't you get my text? I told you we were heading to the children's ward. Thomas wanted to paint.'

'I didn't get any text. I finished up early and I've been searching the whole hospital looking for you.' He pulled his phone out of his pocket and checked it.

Jessie could see the moment he realised he was in the wrong, red blotches breaking out on his cheeks. 'Sorry. I didn't hear it.'

'It's fine. I wouldn't have taken Thomas anywhere without telling you. We just came to get some art supplies but it seems he's found a friend too.'

'I'm not sure crossing professional boundaries will endear me to the staff here. Thomas, let's go,' he said gruffly, grabbing his son's belongings and making Jessie believe she'd really stuffed things up, even though she'd done everything she could to keep Thomas happy.

'I got the sister's permission and he was quite content.' Unlike now, when he seemed agitated at being forced to leave. She knew why Cameron was uncomfortable about her being around his son but it didn't seem fair for their troubled history to impact on those around them.

'Can I do the project now, Dad?' Now that his distraction was being packed away it seemed Thomas's attention was back on the problem which had brought him here in the first place.

'No, sorry, son. I haven't had time to speak to your teacher and I doubt there will be anyone in at this time. I'll phone first thing tomorrow, okay?'

'I want to do the project. It's not fair if I can't win a prize too.' It was clear that Thomas's frustration was beginning to build again. He'd abandoned the picture and the paints he'd been so engrossed in until his father had arrived, his attention totally focused on the project he wasn't being allowed to participate in.

'I know, son. I told you we'll try and sort something out.'

'But you're never at home.' Thomas was in tears again and Jessie felt bad for everyone involved, including Simon, who was quietly watching on. She knew Cameron was devoted to his son, but as a single parent who was also a surgeon he probably couldn't be at home as much as he wanted to be. It was clear Thomas needed extra care and attention but it was equally obvious that it wasn't something easily acquired.

Jessie wanted to help but she was acutely aware that Cameron wasn't completely over their historic break-up. Or, if he was, he simply didn't want to spend any more time around her than was necessary. She was finding their reacquaintance difficult for different reasons and, though they would likely never be as close as they once had been, she could do without seeing that look of betrayal in his eyes every time he spoke to her. Perhaps if she could help him with his current crisis he would see that she wasn't the enemy. That she'd only ever wanted what was for the best.

As they left the ward, Thomas walking ahead, arms folded and doing his best to ignore his father, Jessie ventured to express an idea.

'Tell me to mind my own business if you

wish, but what if you incorporated his love of art into his school project?'

'What do you mean?' Cameron's scowl made her swallow hard, concerned that she was stepping over the line which he had clearly drawn from the moment he'd set eyes on her again.

'The project can be on any subject of his choice, right? Perhaps he could do a study of wildlife or nature using his artistic skills. With such a broad spectrum for the basis of the project, I don't see why he couldn't showcase his talents in such a manner. I'm sure the school would be pleased that he'd be able to participate with the rest of his class-mates and hopefully Thomas would enjoy it too. He showed me his sketchbook and he's really good.'

'He doesn't usually share that with any-one,' Cameron confided, letting her know this was a privilege she shouldn't take lightly, something which had obviously taken him by surprise.

'I take after my mum, Dad says,' Thomas interrupted without a trace of arrogance or yearning for the mother missing from his life, evidently forgetting his vow of silence upon leaving the ward.

Jessie glanced at Cameron for confirmation.

'It's true, Ciara is an artist too. She preferred sitting in her studio alone to spending quality time with her family.' It was clearly a sore point. Perhaps Cameron hadn't mentioned where his son's interest and talent lay because it reminded him of his wife and the end of their relationship.

'Well, I think if you base the project on Thomas's artwork, and add some text on the subject he likes to accompany the illustrations, it could work.' The idea certainly had Cameron thinking, his haste to get away from her now slowing so he could consider the suggestion. Thomas too was listening intently.

'I like birds. Can I do my project on birds, Dad?'

'We'll see, Thomas. I would still have to find someone who could help you. You know there are some nights and weekends when I'll have to come to work and I don't want you to start something if you're not going to be able to finish it.'

'What about Jessie? She could help me.' Thomas looked at them both with such hope and faith that she would be the one to fix this problem that Jessie was rendered speechless, knowing that whatever response she gave would upset one of the Holmes men.

Thankfully, Cameron answered for her. 'Jessie has her own work and family to take care of. I'm sure she doesn't have time to supervise your homework too. I'll see if I can persuade Maggie to help you with it.'

It wasn't surprising that he didn't want her venturing any further into his private life when he'd barely given his consent for her to mind Thomas for that short time this afternoon. Jessie wasn't part of his world any more, apart from the time they were forced to spend together at work, and it seemed as though that was the way he'd prefer to keep it.

'Maggie doesn't like it when I make a mess with the paint and she's no good with homework. I want Jessie.'

It would be difficult to explain to him that the reason she couldn't help him was because they'd been together once and his father couldn't stand to be near her after the way she'd treated him.

'Listen, Cameron, I could maybe spend an hour or two a week helping him. It would solve the problem, and keep him happy.' She knew the last thing either of them wanted was to be forced together for any longer than necessary, but this would be about her helping Thomas. Other than giving his permission, Cameron wouldn't have to get involved.

'I can't ask you to do that,' he said, his forehead furrowed in a frown.

'You didn't. Thomas did.' He was the reason she was even contemplating it, and trying to avoid another meltdown. Along with her need to make amends for all the hurt she'd caused Cameron fifteen years ago, and more recently.

His decision now would tell her once and for all how desperate he was to have her out of his life for good. Only now was she realising that she wasn't ready to lose him again.

* * *

He was stuck. Caught between his son's educational needs and his own wish to keep an emotional distance from Jessie. It had been a tough call even to leave him with her in this afternoon's emergency but doing it on a regular basis seemed like madness. Yes, Jessie's help would solve a lot of problems, but at what cost? Having her around could cause him even more.

He'd been in a real bind today, with no other option but to leave Thomas with her after his upset. However, when he'd come back to find the room empty he'd gone into a tailspin. He didn't know what he'd imagined Jessie had done with his son, only that he didn't want her to hurt Thomas the way she'd hurt him. It was a ridiculous thought, of course. Jessie would never have done anything to put Thomas in any danger, but it was a knee-jerk reaction.

The reason he was trying not to get involved with her again was to avoid that pain she'd managed to inflict on him before. But it wasn't fair to deny his son an opportunity like this when he'd fought so hard for

Thomas to be treated the same as his class-mates. Besides, he remembered how much it had helped him to have Jessie as a study buddy and perhaps it would have the same positive effect on Thomas's work too.

'Well, if you're both sure…' He supposed it wouldn't be for ever, probably only as long as he'd be here for Simon's recovery. Neither was going to be a permanent arrangement, and it would at least help them over this one hurdle for now. He had to look to the future instead of back at the past. Jessie certainly didn't seem to be too concerned about what had gone on between them before. He knew he hadn't wanted to revisit that time with her, but so far there had been no apology or real explanation for what had happened. It was about time he followed her lead and moved on.

CHAPTER FIVE

THIS WAS ASKING for trouble. Cameron knew it and yet he was still walking headlong into the disaster he knew would surely follow.

When the doorbell rang he felt that first date excitement, regardless that this was anything but a romantic liaison. It was home schooling for his son that, despite his complicated history with the person who'd come to assist him, he'd been compelled to accept because he knew she had the patience Thomas required.

'Hi. Where do you want me?' It was such a loaded question from the woman standing on his doorstep.

The answer uppermost in his mind was *As far away as possible*, as he knew being this close to her again had the potential to break his heart all over again. Despite everything she'd put him through, Cameron knew he still had feelings for her. Otherwise it wouldn't be so hard for him to be near her.

After a pause that was slightly too long he said, 'Thomas is in the kitchen at the table.'

Jessie flashed him a smile as he stood aside to let her in.

It was a big deal for Cameron to let someone into his life again, on any basis. Especially someone who'd hurt him and let him down the way Jessie had. He was trusting her not to betray him again, by inviting her into his home and into his son's life too. Although they hadn't had much choice. Jessie couldn't invite him to her home with her ailing mother in residence and a coffee shop or library would have been too distracting for Thomas.

'Hi, Thomas.' Jessie waved and unhooked the backpack she was wearing over her shoulder.

'Thomas, this is Jessie. You remember? From the hospital.'

'Hi, Jessie,' Thomas dutifully acknowledged as he reluctantly set his game console down on the table. They'd had a conversation earlier where Cameron had laid down some ground rules—no games, full concentration, and to be polite to Jessie. All of which were easier said than done with a ten-year-old.

Jessie plonked herself in the seat next to him and began unpacking notebooks and pens onto the table. 'So, Thomas, is there any particular subject you'd like to do your project on?'

'I want to do mine on birds,' Thomas said.

With Jessie's support, Thomas had a fighting chance along with everyone else. Cameron knew from experience. When they'd been revising for exams and he'd struggled to remember details, Jessie had covered the place in brightly coloured notes because she'd read that visual stimulation helped dyslexia sufferers retain information. It was something, along with her tips on mind-mapping, that he'd continued utilising in his medical school studies too.

'There should be some reference books over here you could use.' Glad to be of use in some capacity, Cameron went in search of some bird-related tomes from the shelves in the living room. He gathered as many wildlife books and encyclopaedias as he could carry.

'That's a good start. I'll print out a few things from the Internet for next time.'

'I'm really grateful to you for doing this, Jessie. Thanks again.' Cameron walked away, afraid that he might say or do something he'd come to regret.

It had been a long time since anyone had done something thoughtful for them and it said a lot that it was Jessie who'd come to the rescue. He couldn't help but think there was a reason she'd come back into his and Thomas's lives now. But it was too frightening to dwell on why that might be.

Would it be nice to have a loving, caring partner, someone who would be there for Thomas too? Yes, and yes. The risks involved in thinking that Jessie could be that person, however, were too great to let his imagination run too far ahead of a nice gesture.

He closed the door between the living room and the kitchen, between him and Jessie. Keeping temptation at bay for a little longer and letting her do the job she'd come here to do.

Jessie took a moment to take in her surroundings, the house Cameron had shared with his wife and son. His family home. One which didn't include her.

The house was more than big enough for the two of them, and she wondered if Cameron had planned to have more children. Maybe his wife's reaction to their son's extra needs had ended those plans. She knew he wouldn't have wanted a large family when he'd been lost among his siblings, but he was obviously such a great dad it was a pity he hadn't been given the chance to expand his young family.

If things had been different he would have had two children now. She would never know if they would have eventually worked something out, had she told him about the baby and if it had survived. Now children were no longer an option for Jessie.

She would've loved children, a family of her own, and a husband who would've supported her. Circumstances had made that impossible for her. So, instead, she tried to keep busy at work and looking after her mother at home. Helping Thomas with this project was something different for her to focus on.

It was difficult not to be bitter at times, especially when Cameron had gone on to have that life with someone else. Perhaps if she'd been honest with him instead of trying to fix things the way she'd always done they might have had some sort of relationship, but there was no going back and they had to live with the decision she'd made.

She was being punished for it now, sitting in her ex's stylish home, helping the son he'd been given by another woman with his homework and knowing Cameron didn't want her there.

'We could start with a list of garden birds and write a description of what they look like. What's your favourite?'

'Robins, I guess.' Thomas was swinging his legs and flicking idly through the stack of books Cameron had provided before disappearing.

She knew he was invested in his son's education so she had to put his vanishing act down to having her in the house. It wasn't ideal for either of them, but she was sure it was best for Thomas to meet her in a safe, familiar environment.

So far he didn't seem to have any problems with her but he was having trouble focusing. She supposed, faced with a stack of books and little stimulation, she might have trouble maintaining interest too.

'We could just print out some pictures, but it might be nice for you to do your own illustrations.' It was important to make a connection, to discover his interests and use them to keep him engaged. Sometimes half of the battle when dealing with children this age was keeping their interest and preventing them from becoming bored. She wasn't an expert by any means, but she'd dealt with a lot of paediatric patients and practising physiotherapy on children required a lot of patience and understanding. To get the best results for her and her patients she needed their co-operation, so she always went the extra mile to get it. Whether that included playing their favourite music or watching TV while she worked with them, she did whatever it took to improve their circumstances.

Thomas clearly wanted to participate in the project, so all she had to do was find the best way to channel his concentration. That might not be through copying from a stack of dusty old books.

'Sometimes we go to the beach or to the park and I like to draw there.'

'That sounds lovely.'

His artistic talent was something his parents should have been proudly showing off, but she noticed that none of Thomas's pictures had been displayed on the fridge or anywhere else. If this was her child's amazing artwork she'd have decorated the entire house with it.

She reminded herself that Cameron's personal issues were not her business and focused her attention back on the matter of the school project she was here to assist with.

'I don't want to copy from boring books. Can we go to the park, Dad? Please?' Thomas called to his father, sounding desperate for an escape from the house.

It was entirely Cameron's decision whether or not they went exploring elsewhere, although when he came to the doorway and flicked a glance at her she was compelled to add her opinion.

'It might help Thomas to have first-hand experience rather than simply copying information and illustrations already available. He could put his own spin on things.'

In fact, it could benefit them all if they weren't confined to this house full of memories which didn't include her.

Being a part of Jessie's study session hadn't been in Cameron's plans. He wasn't always going to be around to help with the homework so he'd thought it more prudent to let her get on with it without him. Driving his son to a park wasn't a hardship. It was something he enjoyed, spending time together feeding the ducks and watching the world go by. Today, having Jessie join them, was simply an added dimension to their quality time together—an air of jeopardy. But he knew it would be worth giving up his time and peace of mind to make a start on Thomas's project.

'Do you want me to wait here until you've finished?' It was a last attempt to separate himself from Jessie, to let her get on with the job she'd come to do without him being involved. Even as he asked the question he knew he wouldn't get away scot-free.

'No, Dad, you come too. You can take some photographs.' Thomas immediately found him a job to keep him occupied and be a part of their expedition team.

'I doubt Thomas will be able to sketch everything in real time. We'll have to document his surroundings for future reference. If it seals the deal, I'll buy the hot drinks.' Jessie's bribery tactics worked as he undid his seatbelt and resigned himself to spending the afternoon with his son and his ex-love. Though the promise of an afternoon together only put him on edge. He didn't want a reason to have Jessie go up in his estimation. He wanted to hold on to his anger surrounding the pregnancy he hadn't known about. But that was proving difficult when he was witnessing the lengths she was willing to go to in order to assist his son.

She'd already gained Thomas's trust and found a way to integrate his interests into this school project to make it more fun for him. Not to mention this outing away from the kitchen table to keep Thomas excited about this take on his homework. It had been the right decision, but he'd do well not to let these positive feelings edge out the older negative ones. It was important not to forget how devastated he'd been by her rejection and the pain which had all but ripped his heart in two. He couldn't afford to let history repeat itself when his son was involved now too.

It would be so easy to let her slot into their little family and fill that void Ciara had left, but he'd learned his lesson about getting close too quickly. In his experience it wasn't better to have loved and lost, when he'd been hurt twice over by the women he'd loved.

Both he and Thomas had been rejected and abandoned enough and that was why he donned his armadillo shell when it came to love and relationships now. Not even Jessie could penetrate that armour and cause more internal damage.

'Can I go to the lake and draw the ducks, Dad?' Thomas was bouncing on the balls of his feet, his sketchbook and pencils clutched in his hands, raring to go.

Cameron had never seen him so eager to do any work and it was entirely down to Jessie. She had that knack of engaging others. Though she hadn't had to try that hard with him in their schooldays. He'd been gone since the second she'd asked him if he wanted some help, the only person then who'd ever taken the time to notice him. It helped that she'd been, and still was, gorgeous.

He watched her now as she walked back from the coffee van, the sun shining on her chestnut curls, picking out the reds and golds in her hair like burnished autumn leaves. She turned and smiled at him, her big green eyes shining on him so he felt as though he was the only person in the world, making him forget his son, who was pulling on his shirt reminding him he was there.

Focus, Cameron.

'Uh…just don't go too close to the edge. Stay where I can see you.'

Remind me why I'm here.

Thomas ran off as Jessie carried over the paper cups. 'I treated you to a latte instead of that muddy water they pass as coffee at the hospital.'

'Thanks. Thomas has gone on ahead. I booked us a seat under the tree out of the sun.' It wasn't overly hot, but warm enough that he'd made Thomas put on sunscreen and a hat before they'd left.

'How thoughtful of you to make a reservation. It's definitely a step up from the hospital canteen.'

They both sat down and Cameron tried not to look when her olive-green shirt dress fell open at the knee when she crossed her legs. He didn't need to be reminded of all the times those slender legs had been wrapped around him.

'Simon seems to be doing well.' Desperate to divert his thoughts from places they really shouldn't be going, he chugged back the milky coffee and burned his tongue.

'Yeah. Kids bounce back. I just hope social services can locate some family for him. He's been through enough without ending up in the care system at the end of it all.'

Cameron opened his mouth wide and stuck out his tongue, letting the cool air soothe his scorched tongue. 'He'th a good boy,' he lisped.

Jessie faced him with a frown etched on her forehead. 'Are you okay?'

'I burned my tongue.'

'Idiot—' she laughed '—you never did have any patience.'

For a split second they just stared at each other, the laughter dying away, and he knew she was also thinking of all the good times they'd once had together. If only the moment wasn't spoiled by the reality of how that time had ended, he might have managed to hold his scalded tongue.

'Not when it comes to food or drink. I would've waited for you, though, if I'd been given the chance.' Despite all the promises to himself not to go there, a couple of minutes alone with Jessie and he was spilling his guts.

She looked away. 'Please don't do this, Cameron.'

'Sorry. I just can't help thinking about what could have been.'

Every time I'm with you.

'It's all in the past. Besides, you wouldn't have Thomas if you hadn't gone on without me.'

'I know, but sometimes I think Ciara was simply my rebound. We got married too young, too quickly. I shouldn't blame her for things going wrong. You were a hard act to follow.' He smiled, trying not to make her feel bad, but she refused to look at him.

'Something else I should feel guilty about, I suppose.' She took a sip of coffee, though he suspected she'd rather throw it at him.

He was trying, and failing, to explain why he'd married someone who wasn't her. Even though it was Jessie who'd broken things off, and nothing could come of it anyway, he wanted her to know that he hadn't simply stopped loving her. He hadn't gone off to uni and forgotten about her. Far from it.

'Definitely not. It was entirely my doing. I guess we'd made all those plans together and I carried them with me. I still wanted those things, but it wasn't what other eighteen-year-old students were looking for in a boyfriend. Then I met Ciara after graduation and I thought we were on the same page.'

Until the reality proved too challenging for one half of their partnership.

'At least you found someone, even for a while. You have Thomas and a life together. I'm still living at home with my mother, so who's the loser here?'

'Okay, you win.' He toasted her victory with his cup, attempting some levity so he wouldn't wander too far down that road which only led to heartache over everything he'd unknowingly lost.

Jessie rewarded him with that sceptical side eye.

'Seriously, though, you could still get married and have children of your own. You can make the break from the past if that's what's been holding you back. Unfortunately, no one else can do that for you.'

Now his initial anger was beginning to fade, it finally occurred to him that she'd been holding on to this secret, and guilt, all this time. Although he disagreed with the decision she'd made, he didn't believe she should punish herself for it. Jessie deserved to be with someone who loved her unconditionally, who could give her the family they had missed out on together.

Ultimately, though, she would put others first and continue to deny herself the same love and support she gave to everyone else in her life. That was just who she was.

Neither this conversation, nor the day itself, had gone where Jessie had expected and she wasn't comfortable with the new direction. She kept telling herself that everything they were doing was for Thomas but she was enjoying being out here, sharing the day with his father too. It wasn't her place, she wasn't part of their family and never would be, as this conversation was proving.

'Of course I wanted a family of my own. There's nothing I would have loved more than to get married and have a baby.' She choked down the tears of grief already bubbling up at the thought of the child they should have had together, and for the ones she would never get to have.

'You could walk away from your mother, you know, or at least entrust her care to someone else. No one would blame you for wanting a life of your own.' Cameron misunderstood the reason why she couldn't do all the things he'd been able to do, but correcting him meant telling him the whole truth. She wasn't sure either of them were ready for that yet.

'I look after Mum because she's the only family I have, the only family I'll ever have. It turns out I have the same condition she does—antiphospholipid syndrome. The autoimmune disorder caused the stroke which left her paralysed, and it's the reason I lost our baby.'

'I'm so sorry, Jessie. I didn't give you the chance to explain what had happened before. But you can still have children, right?'

'There's a high chance of miscarriage and I know I can't put myself through that again. Anyway, I've come to terms with it so there's no point in getting maudlin over things we can't change.' She got up and brushed the grass from her dress before walking down to the water's edge to check on Thomas's progress, and put some distance between her and Cameron. And the pity emanating from him.

That was why she hadn't told him before. It was one thing dealing with his anger at her but sympathy would only make her want to cry. She didn't need him to be nice to her when it made things easier if he remained mad at her.

There was nothing she wanted more than a family. It had been a dream, a possibility, once upon a time. Then fate had stepped in and Cameron had gone on to have that family with someone else. It was futile to convince herself otherwise. He wasn't her husband, Thomas wasn't her son and this wasn't her life.

Trying to avoid opening up any more old wounds, she redirected her attention away from Cameron, peering over Thomas's shoulder to see what he'd been working on. There in the middle of the page he'd captured a mother duck and her ducklings cruising along the water.

'Thomas, that's wonderful,' she said, kneeling down so she could see the drawing in detail.

He'd managed to capture the downy fur of the baby ducks with the soft strokes of his pencil, as well as the small concentric circles emanating around them.

'I still have to add some colour,' he said, batting away her compliment as he wet his paintbrush.

Her enthusiasm drew Cameron down to join them.

'Well done, son. Your mother would be proud of you.' He kissed the top of his son's head and the display of fatherly pride choked Jessie up until her throat was raw and her eyes stung with the effort of not crying.

Witnessing the beautiful moment and seeing what a great father he'd become was a privilege, especially knowing what Cameron had gone through. Thomas's mother should have been proud of both of them and Jessie realised the woman had sacrificed just as much as she had. Whether she'd had the best of intentions by leaving them Jessie couldn't say, but Cameron's ex was missing out on a hell of a lot by not being part of this family.

They fell into silence, watching in amazement as Thomas worked quickly, adding splodges of colour here and there to pick out the features. Later they could add some information about the species and their characteristics to make his study as informative as it was aesthetically pleasing.

A group of rambunctious teenage boys suddenly burst through the quiet, kicking a football between them and occupying the space Jessie and Cameron had just vacated. One of the older, taller lads booted the football high, lodging it in the branches of the tree.

'Forbesy, climb up and get that, will you?'

'Why me?' a smaller, curly-haired teen asked, even as he began to traverse the lower branches.

'Because you're more agile, like a cat.'

'Or more obedient and stupid, like a dog,' the nominated ball retriever grumbled.

It was difficult to ignore what was going on when they were being so loud and disruptive during what had been a peaceful interlude. Jessie had one eye on Thomas and one on the teen antics beside them, so she saw the fall before she heard the shout.

'Forbesy' had slipped on the branch he'd been balancing on when he'd thrown the ball down. Time seemed to stand still as she helplessly watched the boy bounce off the bottom branches before landing flat on his back at the base of the tree.

It took a few moments before it registered with him what had happened, not least because he'd clearly been winded by the fall. By the time he cried out in pain his mates were shouting and rushing to his aid, as Jessie alerted Cameron, 'That looks like a really bad fall.'

Telling Thomas to stay put, they rushed over to offer medical help. Several of the footballers were watching, hands behind their heads in disbelief and looking pale, not knowing what to do. The older boy who'd urged him to climb the tree in the first place was trying to get him into a sitting position.

'Come on, mate. I'll help you up.'

'Do not move him!' Cameron yelled, stopping them all in their tracks. 'I need you to take a step back and give him some air.'

'He's a doctor. Your friend's in good hands,' Jessie explained as Cameron knelt down to check on the boy.

'We just have to make sure he hasn't injured his neck or spine in the fall before he's moved.'

'Should...should we call an ambulance?'

Jessie took up a position on the other side of the injured boy, noticing his arm was bent at an odd angle. 'I think that would be best, yes.'

Now the pain was really beginning to kick in, the boy's face was contorted and he was wiggling around, using his feet to try and lever himself up.

'What's your name? I'm Cameron and I'm a surgeon over at the hospital.'

'Jamie. Jamie Forbes.'

'Well, Jamie Forbes, we need you to stay as still as possible until the paramedics get here. I want to stabilise that neck in case of any spinal injuries. I'm sure you'll be fine, but in my job it's important to take precautions.' He was smiling, his voice calm and steady, and Jessie saw first-hand that he was every bit as patient, caring and understanding with his patients as he was with his own son. She'd seen him with Simon but this was further proof that his nurturing nature wasn't limited to within the hospital walls.

Not that she'd doubted him. The years might have passed, circumstances had changed, but he was still the good man he'd always been.

He bundled up his jacket and used it as a makeshift support for Jamie's neck before moving to look at the teen's arm. Jamie was pale as Cameron located the fracture area just below his elbow and checked his pulse, comparing it to the one in the uninjured arm.

'You're going to be okay, Jamie, but I think you've fractured your arm. Are your parents here?'

'No.'

'Okay. I need you to tell me if you can feel this.' Cameron touched his arm gently but Jamie shook his head.

'Can you open and close this hand for me?'

The boy complied with a yelp of pain.

'The paramedics will be able to give you some pain relief when they get here, and they'll need to put a cast on that arm. Your pulse in that arm is weak, suggesting your fracture might be putting pressure on the artery. I'm afraid I'm going to need to straighten it out and immobilise it. Bear with me.'

Cameron rolled his sleeves up and took a strong grip of the arm. 'I need you to brace yourself. Scream and shout all you want, but please try not to struggle. We need to get this bone back in place. It'll be over really quickly, I promise, Jamie.' He gently applied traction in order to align the limb again.

The teeth-grinding sound of the bone being forced back into place was accompanied by Jamie's short, sharp scream. Most of his friends had to turn away, probably glad they weren't the one in his position. Cameron then gathered some nearby fallen branches to improvise a splint and checked his pulse again.

'Good man. The pulse is sounding better, which means there's no disruption to the blood supply going to the limb.'

'You can use this to immobilise the arm.' Jessie pulled off the blue chiffon dragonfly print scarf she'd been wearing from around her neck.

'Thanks.' Cameron met her gaze and she could feel the warmth of his gratitude radiating from his entire being.

She was sure fixing a broken arm was nothing compared to the life-changing operations he performed daily and she'd played a minor role in it. Yet he was looking at her as though she'd been the hero of the day, simply for being there. It made her wonder how long it had been since he'd had anyone's real support.

By all accounts his wife hadn't been there for him, and she knew his family had never been supportive. Cameron deserved so much more. For a man who gave so much, he didn't seem to receive anything in return. With no significant other in her life, she knew a little about that herself. They were two peas in a pod, caring too much for others and getting little in return. She suspected that the only time they'd both felt loved and cherished was when they'd been together.

Okay, he'd had it briefly with his wife, but ultimately she'd betrayed him. Jessie had too, but she'd never stopped loving him. She doubted she ever would.

CHAPTER SIX

'COME ON, SIMON, I know you can do this.'
Jessie was urging him alongside the walking frame, willing him with every cell in her body to take those steps.

His face was scrunched up with the effort of concentration in putting those limbs to work again, but this was a huge milestone for him. The more progress he made, the better the outcome and future prognosis. If he gave up now and accepted his limitations it was doubtful he would ever be fully mobile again and at such a young age that would be a tragedy. Especially when he'd had these early years with full use of his limbs, leading a full life. If he had to go into the care system as well she wasn't sure if he would ever get the same support for a full recovery as he was receiving now with her and Cameron as his cheerleaders. He was here with her in his free time, urging on their patient who was so much more to both of them.

'I want my mummy and daddy,' Simon cried as he struggled to put one foot in front of the other, and Jessie almost joined him. Life had been so unfair to all of them in this small room, but they were doing their best now. She and Cameron wanted to get Simon back on his feet so he could live as full a life as possible. Cameron, although he'd turned her world on its axis once more, had given her something to look forward to every day. Finally sharing all of those secrets which had burdened her for years had made her soul lighter. Seeing him might have made her think too much about the past, about what she'd lost or would never have, but he was undoubtedly the highlight of her day. In between her duties to her patients and her mother, there was always that anticipation of seeing Cameron to fuel her through her day. He was beginning to thaw towards her, perhaps even learning to trust her again, and Jessie wasn't taking it for granted.

Seeing his wariness around her had almost broken her. Now, getting to see him, working with him reminded her every day why she'd fallen in love with him first time around. She'd forgotten what it was to feel alive, her blood pumping so hard through her body she thought her heart would actually explode at the sight of him. Her existence was no longer simply moving from one task to the other, her emotions completely dependent on the mood and circumstances of those she cared for. She had feelings of her own, regardless that she could do nothing about them, pining for a love that she'd thrown away and a family which would never be hers.

Some day, when it came to an end, when Simon moved on and Thomas had completed his project, she would have to come to terms with never seeing him again and return to her lonely life.

From the second he'd appeared back in her world she'd had cause to be concerned, but spending time with him and Thomas, seeing how he'd treated that boy in the park, had confirmed what she already knew to be true. She still had feelings for Cameron.

He was a great father, a compassionate doctor and a great man. His only fault had been loving her. It had hurt them both when they'd parted, but she was sure he wouldn't be ready to make the same mistake again even if she was.

'I know, buddy, but Jessie and I are here for you as long as you need us.' Cameron wrapped his hand around one of Simon's as he slid the frame along the floor, willing his legs to follow.

Jessie loved that he was as sincerely invested as she was in the boy's progress. Simon looked up at Cameron, his respect and admiration for the man who'd given him this chance to even try and walk again shining in his young eyes. He pursed his lips and braced himself on the frame, a renewed determination on his face because of Cameron's support. She had got him this far with his physical rehabilitation, building his strength and confidence along with the means to recover, but motivation and support were equally important.

Having Cameron working alongside her was an extra source of assistance for both her and Simon. If she had this level of teamwork with every specialist for her patients she would see quicker progress and improved recovery rates overall.

'Just a couple of steps, Simon...' she urged.

Simon moved forward, slowly dragging one foot in front of the other.

'That's it. The first steps are the hardest, now we need you to get to the end. You're doing so well.' She was clapping him on, hoping the momentum would carry him along the length of the hallway. It would do so much towards his mental recovery as well as his physical progress, knowing he could walk through the pain if he really set his mind to it.

'When can I sit down?' Simon asked, breathing heavily with the effort.

'As soon as you get to the wheelchair.' Jessie manoeuvred the wheelchair they'd used to transport him from the children's ward to Rehab.

They couldn't push him too hard in case

his body failed him and damaged his morale. He needed to go out on a high.

Simon grunted and propelled himself the last few steps. His face lit up as they smiled and clapped his efforts.

'I did it.'

'You did.' She had to turn away before she made a fool of herself crying over his success, and busied herself getting the wheelchair into place.

Simon all but fell into it, exhausted, red in the face but clearly delighted with himself, and rightly so. It would've been easy to give up after everything he'd been through and had still to face. The exercise and physiotherapy, though necessary to get him walking again, was nevertheless hard work and painful at times. Her adult patients struggled to get motivated and here was a seven-year-old boy who'd just lost his parents pushing himself to the limit. Jessie was proud of him, and Cameron, and herself.

'Good job.' Cameron congratulated him with a high-five.

'We'll take you back to the ward so you can get some rest now, but tomorrow we'll be doing it all over again. The more you practise, the better and easier your steps will become.' Despite her euphoria she needed to warn him that this was the beginning of his journey, not the end. They couldn't get too complacent about his progress and had to keep pushing him further if he was going to gain full mobility.

Cameron helped her to get Simon back into bed and poured him a glass of orange squash. 'Get some sleep, buddy, and we'll be back to see you tomorrow.'

It was such a sweet moment. Jessie almost expected him to kiss the boy on the head the way he did with Thomas when showing affection. That was how caring he came across and how much of a father-figure he was to this orphaned child who had no one in his life.

'Bye, Simon,' she said, voice raspy with emotion.

'I'll see you tomorrow.' He waved. 'Can't wait to walk again,' he said with the biggest grin on his face she'd seen since his admission to the hospital.

That alone made her job, her dedication and lack of a private life worth it.

As they left the ward she could see Cameron's smile growing wider by the second until they were in the corridor and he seemed unable to control his excitement. She mirrored his happy expression.

'Can you believe that just happened?'

Jessie knew he was talking about Simon taking his first steps, but she was equally buoyed at his enthusiasm to try again tomorrow. It meant they hadn't pushed him too far, too quickly, and his enthusiasm to carry on could be the motivation to get him walking unassisted in no time.

'It's amazing how resilient they are at that age.'

'I think you had a lot to do with young Simon finding his feet again, Ms Rea.'

'That wouldn't have been possible without your surgical skills, Dr Holmes.'

'We make a great team.' He high-fived her then pulled her into a hug with a burst of vocal glee.

Jessie's laugh as he wrapped his arms around her to share the excitement turned into a contented sigh as his body enveloped her. That familiar heat and security of his hard chest and strong arms was something she'd missed for so long.

The colleagues celebrating a patient's progress hug soon turned into something else. A longing for the past, a reconnection they'd been dancing around since they'd found each other again, and a yearning for more. Instead of coming to her senses and pulling away, for once Jessie just wanted something for herself—Cameron holding her and pretending that they'd never parted. He didn't attempt to extricate himself either but rested his chin on the top of her head and squeezed her tighter. The confirmation that he might just miss her was sufficient to undo her. They were a good team, they always had been. It was other circumstances which had been the problem. Now those secrets which had ruined their relationship the first time around made being together more impossible than ever. Even if there was any sign that he had any interest in her.

Cameron now knew about the baby, and the syndrome she'd inherited, but that didn't change anything. It only explained her reason for letting him walk out of her life. She wanted the best for him and that still wasn't her, someone who could never give him a family.

Eventually Cameron's grip on her loosened and they took a step away from each other. He didn't let go of her arms though and when she looked up at him his eyes were staring at her mouth. She watched him dip his head in slow motion to claim her lips with his. It was a mistake, a stupid move which would only serve to make things more awkward and complicated between them.

Yet she didn't try to stop it happening. Her eyes fluttered shut and she gave herself over to that feather touch of his lips brushing hers. How she'd missed this, missed him, missed being loved. Later she could blame her loneliness, her nostalgia and regret, for letting her defences down. She purposely avoided relationships to dodge family complications and guilt, and Cameron embodied everything she should be resisting instead of embracing, but it had been too long and this felt so good.

This kiss was not the hard passion of infatuated teens but a tender longing for one another which brought tears to her eyes. She was almost thankful when they heard chatter coming from around the corner, causing them to break apart and end the beautiful, painful moment.

As tears fell silently down her cheeks, washing away her initial happiness, Jessie turned on her heel and ran from him. It was too heartbreaking, too unfair to be continually reminded of the life, the love, the man she could've had if she'd been braver.

Cameron was pacing the kitchen floor like a first-time expectant father, not sure what to do with himself. Jessie was due to come and help Thomas tonight but, after what had happened between them at work, he couldn't be sure she'd turn up, much less talk to him.

He'd messed up, given in to that temptation to hold her, kiss her, and pretend everything was okay. After hearing about her health issues he'd stopped blaming her for everything that had gone wrong. She hadn't asked for it any more than he had. In true

Jessie fashion she'd been trying to take care of him, protect him from potential harm. Of course she'd been wrong and he would remain devastated that she'd locked him out of that difficult time, but he'd forgiven her.

It was hard to stay angry at her when she proved every day how kind and caring she was. And he'd begun to realise those strong feelings he'd had weren't just about the past. He was still attracted to her and he'd foolishly acted on it. Sure, she'd folded right into his arms and appeared content to be there, but crying and running away after he'd kissed her was not the sign of a good time.

He brushed his hand through his hair for the thousandth time, resisting the urge to pull it out, or do damage to the nearest inanimate object instead. He needed his hands in one piece to do his job and he'd let enough people down for one lifetime. Namely, Jessie.

She'd been honest about steering clear of relationships, and the reason why—the same explanation she'd given for breaking things off with him. Yet sharing the achievement of Simon's first steps with her had given him a false sense of intimacy with her. Why else would he have kissed her in their place of work, not only crossing the line in their friendship but potentially endangering their jobs too?

He swore loud enough for Thomas to pull his headphones off and look up at him from the table.

'It's fine. I stubbed my toe, that's all.' He could add lying to his son to the list of his recent misdemeanours.

Whether Jessie had wanted him to kiss her or not, and despite his longing for her, he shouldn't have done it. His action had jeopardised not only Simon's recovery at the hospital if she decided she could no longer work with him, but also his son's progress. If she didn't feel safe around him there was no way she would come to his house.

He checked his phone. There were no missed calls or new messages and she should've been here fifteen minutes ago. He walked out of the back door to mutter another expletive out of earshot of his impressionable offspring. If he'd ruined all the hard work they'd done to improve the lives of the two boys he'd never forgive himself.

It was only when he heard the knock at the front door he was able to stop beating himself up, though he knew he had some grovelling to do before she'd forgive him.

He hot-footed it back through the house, only to be overtaken by his eager son, clutching his sketchpad. Thomas yanked the front door open and immediately shoved the picture of the park swans he'd been working on in her face.

'Hello to you too, Thomas. Glad to see you've been working away on your own. May I come in?'

Thankfully, Cameron could hear the smile in Jessie's voice, even if he couldn't see it with a drawing pad obscuring her from view. She didn't sound as though she'd come here to slap him with a lawsuit or a restraining order.

'Let Ms Rea in, Thomas.' Cameron rested his hands on his son's shoulders and gently ushered him aside to allow Jessie access to his home.

'Ms Rea, is it now?' She cocked an eyebrow at him, one corner of her mouth curved upward in the tease.

Relief flowed out of him in one short heavy breath. 'I wasn't sure if you'd even come tonight after…you know…' He squirmed, facing her like that awkward teenage boy who'd kissed her when they were supposed to be revising—moving in, caught up in how close she was sitting next to him, only to plant his lips on the end of her nose instead of her mouth. They'd laughed about it then before he'd made a successful second attempt, which was imprinted on his brain and his lips for ever.

'I did think about it. Not showing up, I mean, but that wouldn't have been fair on Thomas.'

'I know. I'm so sorry. Please forgive me.'

'What for?' She was going to make him spell out his transgression in minute detail to make sure he'd never do it again.

'For kissing you without permission. I'm truly sorry. I don't want to ruin things for Simon and Thomas because of my foolish, selfish actions.'

Now it was her turn to look puzzled, evidently confused by the words.

'What made you think I wasn't a willing partner? Was it the snuggling into your chest or the kissing you back?'

'No, it was the crying and running away.'

'Oh. Oh! You saw that, huh?'

'Yes, and I've been kicking myself ever since. Are you telling me I got it wrong?' He was struggling to comprehend an alternative explanation for the abrupt departure.

Jessie pressed a hand to his chest and sighed. 'I missed this, Cameron. I miss you, but we both know it would only end in tears again. As proven today.'

'Wow. So let me get this straight… You wanted me to kiss you?' That made him see the incident in an altogether different light. It hadn't been the disastrous act of a desperate man crossing the line but the culmination of a mutual attraction and want for one another.

Jessie bunched his shirt in her hand and pulled him down so his face was a breath away from hers. 'I wanted you to kiss me, I liked it, and I'd love to do it over and over again.'

To illustrate her point, she pressed her lips against his and lingered there for a brief moment before he could fully enjoy the sensation.

'But neither of us are in a situation to take this any further, so I suggest we put it behind us and concentrate on the boys' needs rather than our own.'

She let go of him and sauntered past towards the kitchen, leaving Cameron reeling from another all too brief intimacy. In the three years since Ciara had left he hadn't even looked at another woman. Now, with Jessie on the scene, he seemed to have become some sort of sex maniac because being with her was all he could think of, wanting what they used to have together before complications beyond his control got in the way.

Far from putting his mind at ease, the knowledge that Jessie wanted him too was only going to make things even more unbearable. Look but don't touch had always seemed a particularly cruel rule to him.

Jessie was flushed with her bravado and the feel of having Cameron pressed against her again, if only for one more precious second. She'd agonised over coming tonight, knowing it was leading her straight into the path of temptation—a dangerous journey she apparently couldn't resist.

In the end she'd thought of Thomas's little face and the prospect of having to disappoint him. If left to finish the project alone, he might never find the motivation. Just like Simon, he needed her support and his needs had to come before hers.

She'd convinced herself that coming to Cameron's house was the right thing to do for his son, the selfless path. Except within a heartbeat of seeing Cameron again she was mauling him and trying to snog him senseless. Thank goodness for a ten-year-old distraction.

'Hey, Thomas, how's the project looking?' She sat down and sorted through the loose sheets of paper currently covering the table.

'Okay, I guess. It's not the same working from photographs. I can't get the stupid colours right.' He didn't sound as bright as he had been since they'd started working the art angle on the project.

'I'm sorry, Thomas, but I can't take you to the park every day. I have work and by the time I get home sometimes it's too dark.' Cameron joined them at the table. Even when he could be taking a time out with Jessie there to take the reins for a while, he still wanted to be a part of everything. He was a much better parent than his own had been.

Jessie guessed the photographs that Thomas was working from had been printed out from Cameron's phone. He'd made the effort to snap the birds at some point during his working day as he couldn't spend the whole afternoon there with his son. She understood Thomas's frustration but she could also see how much he was loved by his father, who was doing his best in difficult circumstances.

'You're always at stupid work. It's not fair,' Thomas lashed out, swiping the jar of water containing his dirty brushes over the table.

Jessie gasped as a river of muddy water

sloshed across his sketches and the printed photographs. She grabbed the pictures closest to her while Cameron's quick reflexes managed to rescue the rest. However, the torrent of water had cascaded over the sides of the table into Jessie's lap.

'Thomas, look at the mess you've made,' Cameron chastised. It was the first time Jessie had ever heard him raise his voice, but he was crouching at eye level, trying to get Thomas to understand that his behaviour was unacceptable without being intimidating or threatening.

'I think we've saved most of it,' she said, standing up to show them the drawings she'd salvaged, water dripping down her legs.

'But you're soaked through.'

'I'll live.'

'Sorry, Jessie.' Thomas hung his head and it was obvious he regretted his outburst so she saw no need to make him feel worse.

'No harm done. My clothes will dry out, but I think we should set your drawings somewhere to do the same while we clean this mess up.'

Between them they set to work mopping up the spilled water and setting aside Thomas's completed pictures. His work in progress had suffered the most damage, but Jessie hoped that once it dried out he would still be able to use it.

It had been an unexpected outburst but thankfully they had managed to defuse it quickly. They both had some experience dealing with such behaviour but she could see why some people found it too challenging to be around. She'd had patients throw furniture at her, directing their fear at her. It took strength and patience to deal with incidents like this. It was a shame that Thomas's mother hadn't been able to.

'I think perhaps we'll set the drawings aside for a while and concentrate on the text. It'll be better for you to put the information down in your own words, so I thought you could read some relevant articles and watch some documentary clips.'

She'd loaded her digital tablet with some videos since he seemed to enjoy his screen time. A now calm Thomas plugged in his earphones and Jessie set a notepad and a pencil beside him so he could take notes.

'That should keep him occupied for a while,' she told Cameron, who was washing the paintbrushes and the jar at the kitchen sink.

'You're so good with him. He listens to you. Sometimes tempers flare and the whole thing escalates, but you handle him better than some of his teachers. And his mother.'

It was a compliment of sorts, but it couldn't lift the sadness around the family circumstances here. Jessie wasn't going to be around for long and they would all do well to remember that.

'He's a good boy, you know that, and it just takes a bit of time for others to see that. This was nothing. Just the average pre-teen having a tantrum.' She gestured towards her stained shirt and jeans.

He looked sheepishly at her. 'I'm so sorry. You're soaked. I should've offered you a change of clothes.'

'Honestly, it's not necessary—'

'I can't let you sit in wet clothes. I'm sure there's something you could change into.'

She followed him to the main bedroom,

which was odd on so many levels when they'd agreed not to blur those lines again.

The décor had clearly been his wife's choice, with a cherry blossom and hummingbird theme decorating the pale blue walls. He opened one side of the wardrobe and Jessie was confronted with rails of shirts and suits. When he opened the other door, however, it was empty save for the coat hangers.

She'd half expected to find evidence of his wife still there, the bottom of the wardrobe filled with shoes, perhaps the top shelf loaded with handbags. As though he was waiting for her to come back and pick up where she'd left off with her family.

'She went to work one day and just never came home. All I got was a text message to say she'd left us and wouldn't be coming back, that our marriage was over, followed by a voice message saying that she wanted a divorce. No discussion, no mention of our son, she simply abandoned us and her life here,' Cameron confided, as though picking up on her train of thought.

There'd been times in the past when she'd

wished she could do the same, walk away from everything to reinvent herself somewhere else. The difference was that she'd never had the courage to act. She had some appreciation for what Ciara must have been going through to have taken such drastic action, but would never understand her walking away from her family in such a brutal fashion.

Even breaking things off with Cameron all those years ago had eaten away at her conscience, guilt and regret shadowing her every decision since. She wondered if Ciara ever doubted the decisions she'd made, or ever thought about coming back.

Jessie shivered, the ghost of Cameron's ex haunting her even though she hadn't been a fixture in his life for years. Although Cameron had been hurt she couldn't be certain he wouldn't welcome Ciara's return if faced with the opportunity.

'I'll see if I can find something less formal and more comfortable for you to wear.' He left her in the room, closing the door behind him.

Jessie began to strip off the wet clothes

sticking to her skin. She tossed her shirt on the bed and was wriggling out of her jeans when Cameron burst back into the room.

'I found these in the spare room. They still have the tags on so I don't think they've been worn...' He came to a halt, the armful of clothes now falling onto the floor as he found her half undressed in his bedroom.

'Sorry, I should've knocked,' he said without taking his eyes off her, standing in nothing but her underwear.

He'd seen her in a lot less, but she liked seeing this look of desire darkening his eyes, letting her know he still wanted her even if circumstances forbade it.

'It's your house.' She shrugged and closed the distance between them to retrieve the clothes he'd brought, though she made no move to put them on.

Cameron bent down to pick up the T-shirt and tracksuit bottoms he'd brought and she saw the stiff way he lowered himself to the ground and the hand which flew to the small of his back when he tried to stand again.

'You were serious about getting that back

massage?' she said as she pulled on the over-sized leisurewear he'd provided.

'I'm fine. Being on your feet for hours of surgery can play havoc sometimes, that's all.'

'You need to get that seen to. It's only going to get more painful otherwise.'

'I don't have time. I'm sure it'll work itself out.' Men, and particularly doctors, made the worst patients as they were too stubborn to acknowledge they had a problem and seek help.

Jessie rolled her eyes. Uncooperative patients were a daily hazard of her job, until they realised that her 'stupid exercises' and 'intrusion' into their personal space improved their physical ailments.

'Back pain never "works itself out". It's a sign there's something wrong, or that you simply need to improve your posture. Bad habits can have a detrimental effect on your physical wellbeing. It's down to me to re-train people's way of thinking or, in your case, standing.'

His look told her all she needed to know about how much she was annoying him be-

cause she was right and all the more determined to prove her worth as a fellow medical
professional. She might have gone down a
different route, wasn't perhaps regarded as
highly as her more qualified peers, but it
didn't make her role any less important.

The patients needing the most hospital
care often had a multi-disciplinary team of
experts working together to get them back
to the best health possible. She was a part
of that team and needed as much as the doctors, surgeons, counsellors or dietitians.
When the injuries had been operated on,
when people were working on getting their
physical strength back, she was the one there
pushing and cheering them on to recovery.
She never let something as minor as a dis-
agreeable personality get in the way.

Cameron seemed so determined to keep
her at arm's length she thought he'd rather
crawl into work on hands and knees than
ask for her help.

As he turned to leave, the awkward angle
he'd twisted his body into clearly exacer-
bated whatever was already ailing him as
he cried out.

'Cameron?' Jessie rushed to him as he muttered an expletive.

'I can't straighten up.' His face was contorted in pain, his breathing shallow, as he fought through the pain.

'Take deep breaths while we get you over to the bed.' In different circumstances she wouldn't have been so bold, might even have blushed at the unintentional innuendo, but she was more concerned with Cameron's back spasm. If he was out of action he wouldn't be able to keep seeing Simon, and as a result would be missing from her working days—his presence was the one thing she had to look forward to between her responsibilities. In short, she had to help Cameron so she could continue to get her regular fix of grumpy ex-boyfriend who only tolerated her because he had to.

She was beginning to suspect she had issues of her own.

'I don't want to hear *I told you so* either,' he grumbled as she helped him over to the bed.

'As if I would.' She feigned innocence when they both knew that was exactly what she wanted to say. Her competitive nature was what had got them both through their exams. They'd each challenged the other to be the best, comparing scores and teasing the loser, when in reality she'd been secretly pleased when his grades had surpassed hers. There had been something about seeing a happy Cameron that she'd found addictive. That was why it would've proved soul-destroying to ruin his life by tying it to hers for ever. It had been hard enough seeing him upset when she'd ended their relationship. She'd had to console herself with the thought that he would smile again once he'd achieved his dream, even if she'd cried herself to sleep more times than she cared to remember.

'Ouch,' he complained as she helped him into a sitting position on the edge of the bed.

'You were never a good patient.'

'You made an excellent nurse, as I recall.' Despite his obvious pain, Cameron managed to give her that dangerous *I remember what we got up to the last time we played doctors and nurses* look.

'Yes, well, we were young and stupid,' she said.

As nice as it sometimes was to remember being curled up in his bed together, blocking out the rest of the world from their little love nest, it wasn't going to do her any favours now.

Cameron was divorced, a father, a surgeon, and they had nothing in common except the pain of their past and the children they were helping. It would be foolish to wish for anything more when her circumstances hadn't changed.

Yet his blue eyes were still watching her with something more than interest in what she was doing. If she wasn't imagining it there was a longing there. Whether it was for something more now or for back then she couldn't tell.

'Shirt. Off. Now.' Her voice was so thick with that same yearning she could barely get the words out, never mind arrange them into a coherent sentence.

He started to unbutton, his eyes never leaving hers as he did so. Mouth dry, she wet her lips with a sweep of her tongue and saw the brilliant blue bloom of his irises darken to midnight.

Jessie positioned herself between his legs in order to help him out of his shirt. It was something she'd done countless times for her patients but never had it felt so intimate.

'You're very authoritative when you want to be.' The corners of his mouth tilted up into a smile as he watched her up close. Too close, she realised too late. When she'd pushed the shirt over his shoulders it left her nowhere to go but closer, until she managed to clear it from his muscular torso. By which point she was practically pushing her chest into his face while having a good feel of his biceps as she undressed him.

'I'd never get anything done otherwise,' she countered in an attempt to disguise the lust currently doing the fandango through her entire being.

In his late teens Cameron had been wiry and lean, limbs strong and long enough to wrap around her and make her feel safe. Now Cameron had filled out in all the right places until muscles visibly popped and chest hair comprised of more than a few straggly follicles.

'I need you face down. So I can work on your back,' she explained, to cover her wandering mind.

He smirked before gingerly turning over on to the bed to let her breathe a sigh of relief. Perhaps she could do her job more efficiently and professionally if he wasn't scrutinising her every move, looking at her the way he used to do when she was trying to study, until she'd been able to resist no longer, forced to admit to the chemistry between them when they were together in a room.

With a deep breath she rubbed her hands together before laying them on Cameron for the first time in years.

His skin was warm, his muscles rigid, as she moved her way deftly down his torso.

'Try and relax. I'm not going to hurt you. Much.' She attempted to bring some levity to the situation, to break the tension she felt under her fingers and in the air.

'It's the "much" I'm worried about,' he grumbled into the duvet cover.

Doing her best to focus on where she was needed, on treating him as a patient rather than an ex-boyfriend, Jessie kneaded and manipulated the tight knots she found under his skin, praying they'd both come out of this unscathed, maybe even recovered.

This was torture. It felt good, too good in fact, to have Jessie's hands on him again, but torturous all the same.

The way Jessie was working her magic on his back felt like an intimate, sensual act they'd participated in when they'd been lovers, making him feel things other than muscular relief. He hadn't helped himself by bringing up memories of the time when she'd nursed him through a nasty flu. With his family oblivious, calling him a drama queen, she'd been the one cooling his brow and bringing him soup. Okay, he might have prolonged his illness for that very reason, enjoying the attention, but they'd both benefitted in the end. He'd repaid Jessie's kindness over and over again when he'd recovered.

Given the chance to do things over again,

he would have fought harder to keep her in his life all those years ago. He would rather have had her in his life above all else and it would have saved him the heartache of trying to replicate their relationship with someone who clearly wasn't Jessie.

'Are you okay? I don't think I've ever had such a quiet patient.' Jessie stopped the massage to check on him.

He couldn't tell her he was focusing hard on not enjoying her touch too much. Groans of appreciation would not have been appropriate in the circumstances. Regardless that her technique was primarily stretching out knots and not for pleasure, he was enjoying the pounding she was giving him.

'Sorry, I was just thinking about my surgery tomorrow.'

Liar.

Jessie tutted. 'You need to take better care of yourself. I'm going to work on some exercises for you to stretch out that back and improve your posture in the meantime. Do you think you can sit up again?'

Cameron tested his neck muscles, first

turning his head so he could look at her. 'So far, so good.'

She took a step back, giving him some room to push himself back up into a sitting position. 'Good. You look a bit more flexible.'

He slipped his shirt back on and stood to stretch out his back a bit more. 'That seems much better. Thank you.'

'No problem.'

Having Jessie back in his life was confusing and disruptive. It was also playing havoc with his schedule when he was putting in more hours at her hospital currently than anywhere else in the hope of seeing more of her.

In a parallel universe they might have rekindled that teenage love. He'd realised that he still harboured wants and needs involving Jessie during their impromptu physio session. It didn't help when he'd caught her staring at him half naked, that lingering look telling him she was still interested.

If there was one thing he didn't need it was knowing that Jessie might be having regrets about ever ending things between them.

'Is this another one of those moments where I want to kiss you as much as you want me to?' he asked with a grin, pulling her towards him, finally giving in to those urges.

'You know, waiting for me to give you verbal consent really takes all the spontaneity out of it. I was half naked in your bedroom after all.' Jessie knew this was what she'd wanted from the second she'd decided to come over this evening.

'It's been a while. Sometimes I miss the signals.' He grinned as he swooped in to kiss her, an intensely passionate assault on her lips she hadn't expected but which made her body go languorous in his arms. This was how she remembered it with Cameron. It hadn't been the misremembered fantasy of a broken-hearted teen after all.

If their earlier encounter had been a gentle reintroduction to one another, this was fifth date, let's get it on unbridled wanting. They never could get enough of one another. After that first fumbled kiss things between them had quickly heated up. They'd been each other's first and only until she'd messed things up and sent him into the arms of another woman. Now she realised why no one else had ever come close to Cameron Holmes. No other man had been so demonstrative in their want for her, unafraid to give themselves completely to her the way Cameron did. The way he was doing now.

His warm hands on her back drew her towards him so that her breasts were pushed torturously close against his chest, the thin fabric between them too much to bear.

It was Cameron who called a halt this time, breaking off the kiss to rest his forehead against hers, his short breaths warming her lips where his had been only seconds before.

'I thought we couldn't do this again?'

'We can't,' she replied, her own breath as shaky as the rest of her body at this unexpected display of passion.

'Why is that again?'

'History, your ex-wife, my mother, your son…'

'Ah, yes.' It took the mention of Thomas

for him to back away. 'I should go and check on him and leave you alone.'

He began to walk away but Jessie couldn't resist one last tease. 'If you insist.'

A growl and a stride later he'd taken her back in his embrace for a last lingering smooch. Then he took off again, leaving Jessie a quivering wreck, her body aching for more of him while her brain was yelling at her to run away.

As she pressed her fingers to her kiss-swollen lips she was beginning to think that playing it safe wasn't as much fun as the alternative.

CHAPTER SEVEN

'THANKS FOR COMING.' Cameron hadn't been sure whether to give Jessie a hug or a kiss and ended up settling on an awkward handshake. Things between them had been odd to say the least since they'd kissed—something which had been happening too often, yet somehow not often enough.

He wanted to kiss her every time he laid eyes on her, which was virtually all the time when he was seeing her at work in the hospital and at home when she was helping Thomas. He must have the patience of a saint not to have made another move that evening when he'd found her undressed in his bedroom, when she'd looked at him with the same hunger he was afraid would destroy their common sense again.

It was obvious that neither the chemistry

nor the attraction had dissipated between them but, unfortunately, the timing still wasn't right. If it would ever be. Every time he touched her the world around them disappeared so all that was left was that longing for one another. A dangerous, selfish desire which would impact their real lives so much they shouldn't be playing with fire this way. It would be too risky to put his trust in her when there was every possibility that she could leave him again. He'd been through that too many times to put his faith in another relationship. But that tangible energy between them bubbled and hissed whenever they were in the same room, like water boiling in a pot that was going to spill over at some point and cause a hell of a mess.

With Thomas's project complete it should've been the time to walk away, especially when Simon was improving every day too. He couldn't really justify the amount of time he was spending with one patient any more and it was a good thing that the boy's recovery had gone so well after surgery. But Cameron was afraid if they lost that connection through the boys they would never see each other again and he wasn't ready to say goodbye.

That was why he'd extended an invitation to her tonight.

'I couldn't miss it, could I? Not when our little artist has worked so hard to be part of this.' Jessie put an arm around Thomas as they made their way into the school assembly hall, looking every inch the proud parent as Cameron was.

They'd pulled together as a team to get the school project completed. In order to avoid temptation he'd taken Thomas on more field trips without his tutor but she'd certainly been a big part of helping him finish the work. The result was a beautifully illustrated study of birds in their natural habitats, which would've been at home on any coffee table.

What they'd achieved together made Cameron wonder what their lives would've been like if Jessie had come into it sooner. If she'd never left his life. Jessie's return had filled that hole in his heart which had been there from the day he'd left for medical school without her, but the longing for the life they could've had together remained.

When they were together they were like a little family. If they weren't careful, they could all start to believe that was what they were. But, just as had happened in the past, one day the bubble could burst. It wasn't just his heart on the line any more.

'Dad, are you listening? I said this is the work my class did.' Thomas took him by the hand and led him around the perimeter of the room. The sound of squeaky rubber soles echoed around the walls as his classmates trailed their parents to see the products of their work but Cameron was sure no other child had had the same input from the adults in their lives. He and Jessie had willed him to succeed just as much as they had Simon. Thomas had given them reason to work together, and now it was over they were going to have to make a decision. Did they go back to their separate lives, forever mourning their lost love, or for once in their lives do something for themselves and act on their feelings?

'These are all really good,' Jessie praised as they stopped briefly to glance at the competition, then bent down to whisper in

Thomas's ear, 'But they don't come any-where close to how brilliant yours is.'

Cameron wasn't really paying attention to the others when there was only one project he was interested in. 'Where's yours, Thomas?'

After all the time and effort put into it, and the fact that he hadn't expected to even participate, he expected his son's work to be front and centre of the exhibited work.

'Mine's in the corner, Dad, over there.'

'Look at this one, Cameron—someone's done their project on eighties and nineties cartoons.' Jessie paused by one table sporting a display of badly drawn animations, but he grabbed her by the arm and pulled her towards Thomas's project instead.

'We don't want to show too much interest in his competitors' stuff. Is there anything we can do to draw more attention here?' On Jessie's advice, Thomas had decorated his table with some extra sketches he hadn't used. Cameron made a promise to himself that once they were returned he'd have them framed and proudly displayed around the house.

The sound of Jessie's laugh drew him back to the present.

'What's so funny?'

'You. You've turned into a competitive dad all of a sudden.'

Thomas and Jessie were both grinning at him, but he knew how it felt to put your work out there and not have support. Even when people had stopped laughing and calling him stupid, he'd never had his parents there to share any of his achievements or support him. He wouldn't apologise for being invested in his son's work because when Jessie was gone he would be the only one left to champion him.

'I'm proud, that's all. Now, let's get some photographs. Thomas, you stand there with your project book open so I can see your paintings. Jessie, could you stand next to him?'

'You don't need me ruining your pictures,' she protested, but Cameron wanted a record of her involvement too, in case he never got to see her again.

'If it wasn't for you we would never have

got this finished, so no more pretending otherwise.'

'It was Thomas who did all the work. All I did was give him a nudge in the right direction.' She slowly inched herself closer to Thomas until she was in the frame and Cameron snapped the shot.

'Well, we're very grateful for all your nudging, aren't we, Thomas?'

'Yeah. Let me take a photograph of you and Jessie, Dad.'

'I don't think…'

'Please. I know how to do it.'

He couldn't say no to his son after all the hard work he'd done. It was only one quick photograph to keep him happy. So he handed his phone over and took his place beside Jessie in front of the display table. He put his arm around her and he heard the change in her breathing at the same time his pulse seemed to skip a beat. They smiled for the camera and leaned closer than they needed to, held on to one another longer than strictly necessary.

That was when Cameron knew he didn't want this to be goodbye. She was part of their lives, and they owed it to one another to at least give this a chance. He wanted to kiss her right now and tell her he was willing to bury the past and try again, but now wasn't the time. Not in front of Thomas. It was too early for him to think they were in a relationship, even if that was exactly what Cameron was hoping for.

'Ladies and gentlemen, could you please take your seats.' During their little photo op the headmaster had taken to the stage to speak.

'I guess we should go and get a good viewing spot. Good luck, buddy.' Cameron slapped his son on the back and he and Jessie hurried to get a seat near the front of the audience. Thomas and the rest of his classmates walked up on the stage and waited to hear the results of the prize-giving.

'I know I'm biased but I think he's got a really good chance of winning something.' Excitement was emanating from Jessie. Cameron was trying to keep a lid on his own in case they were all disappointed, but as she clutched on to his arm he could feel that positive energy and couldn't fail to be infected by it.

'As long as it's not something patronising like a participation award, I'll be happy,' he said, having not entirely given up his err on the side of caution stance.

Jessie nudged him, forcing him to smile back, and they both sat on the edges of their seats, waiting for the results to be announced.

'A warm welcome to all parents, children and friends of the school to our very special prize-giving ceremony. Our senior school have been working very hard on their individual projects and I'm blown away by the level of creativity and talent we've seen here tonight.' He turned and began a round of applause for the beaming students sitting behind him, which the audience continued.

'We're going to start with our year eights…'

Cameron and Jessie clapped and congratulated the winners along with the other parents until they reached Thomas's group.

Eyes trained on the stage, Jessie reached for his hand and clutched it tight. Whether she knew it or not, her love for his son was there in her worried expression and need to be held. They could keep pretending they were protecting themselves by not acknowledging their true feelings for one another but the damage had already been done.

'In third place… Max Shriver's *History of the British Royal Family.*'

Another anxious round of applause.

'In second place…' Jessie squeezed his hand tighter '… Angela Robinson's project on *The Ocean Around Us.*'

This time Jessie let go of his hand, clearly feeling as deflated as he was, realising the odds weren't in Thomas's favour.

'There's always next time,' he said, only to be met with a sad puppy look. They both knew there wasn't going to be a next time unless one of them was brave enough to take the next step beyond guilty snatched kisses.

'Jessie, I think we should talk…'

'And first prize goes to *A Study of Birds* by Thomas Holmes.'

Jessie's yelp as she leapt off her seat alerted him to the news before the announcement actually sank in. Thomas had won. Cameron was on his feet too, clapping and hollering at his beaming son as he accepted his first prize trophy.

'He won. I don't believe it.' Cameron thought his heart would burst, it was stuffed so full of pride and love at watching his son's achievement. All of the hard work and perseverance had paid off. He knew Thomas could do everything his classmates could, it just took a little more support to get him there—something which would never be in short supply as long as Cameron had breath in his body.

'He's amazing. You did a good job raising him, Cameron.' Another female voice to the right of him drew his attention. When he saw who it was speaking, clapping Thomas's success as though she deserved to be part of it, the world beneath Cameron's feet seemed to crumble to dust.

'Ciara? What are you doing here?' His head was spinning as that painful part of his life where his wife had left him to bring up their son alone collided with the present, just as he was making progress.

Jessie snapped her head around too at the mention of his ex's name and he saw the euphoria of the moment die on her face. Ciara had spoiled everything.

Coming face to face with Cameron's ex-wife was everything Jessie had dreaded. Ciara was everything she wasn't—super-model tall, slim and elegant. It was difficult not to compare her fun rainbow-print dress, bright pink tights and sneakers to the cream tailored dress and heels the woman on the other side of Cameron was wearing. If she'd known there was a remote possibility of running into her, Jessie would've spent longer getting ready. She might have gone to a hairstylist so there wasn't a stray lock out of place instead of simply bunching it up in an unruly ponytail. It was silly to view this woman as competition when she wasn't with Cameron, and Ciara had more right to be here than Jessie, but that didn't mean she wasn't envious. She'd had the years with Cameron that Jessie should've had, been married to him and had a child with him. Cameron had chosen her and he hadn't been the one to end the marriage.

The odds were not in her favour.

'You sent me a text, remember? I'm sorry I didn't reply, but I wasn't sure if I'd be welcome or not. I'm glad I made it on time.' Ciara's explanation for her sudden appearance didn't do anything to make Jessie feel any less of an intruder. Cameron had invited her. Even after years apart and a divorce, he had wanted her to be a part of this. Jessie's fragile heart broke a little more.

'Thomas asked me to send you a message. You're still his mother.'

With the prize-giving over and the other parents and guests beginning to make their way out, the mini drama was beginning to look a tad conspicuous, with Jessie hovering on the periphery. It wasn't as though he'd introduced her as anyone significant and she didn't think he'd even notice if she left.

'Jessie? Where are you going?'

She was wrong.

'You have family stuff to sort out. Congratulate Thomas for me.' Head down so he wouldn't see the devastation on her face, knowing she didn't stand a chance with him after all, Jessie left the hall.

She'd convinced herself lately that it was

only a matter of time before they caved and gave in to that crazy chemistry she'd believed had grown stronger by the day. Their time together, no matter how short, was always full of that good sort of tension. The kind that could only be relieved when they got to rip each other's clothes off. She should've known when she'd been standing almost naked in his bedroom and it had only prompted a kiss that they weren't going to embark on the raging love affair she'd imagined on lonely nights. It was for the best, she supposed, when she had her mother to look after, and he had his family.

'Jessie, wait.'

She ignored his half-hearted plea, glad she'd come in her own car tonight so she could make a quick getaway. Though he hadn't tried too hard to get her back, staying to talk to Ciara rather than chase after her.

As she stood in the car park she could see the family reunion taking place in real time. An elated Thomas clutching his shiny silver prize was proudly leading his mother over to see his award-winning work, with Cameron following closely behind. She wasn't even an afterthought now the real matriarch was back on the scene. As Jessie watched the happy trio through the window she realised she'd merely been a stand-in until Ciara came to her senses and claimed her rightful place.

It was too late now for Jessie to admit she'd wanted more with Cameron than unbearable sexual tension. Despite her loyalty to her mother, she'd still found the time to be with Thomas, and Cameron, so she'd begun to wonder if maybe they could have tried to make things work. Yes, they still had issues and responsibilities making things difficult for them, but their feelings for one another had been just as strong. Or so she'd thought. One appearance from his ex and she was watching from the outside like a poor kid staring in at a candy store, looking at all the goodies she couldn't have.

Cameron said something that made Ciara laugh and a stabbing pain almost doubled Jessie in two at the sight. When he placed his hand in the small of her back, the way he did with Jessie, she had to look away. It felt so much like a betrayal when that small gesture to her always meant a reassurance that he was there with her. Until now.

She got into the car knowing she would be driving away from Cameron and Thomas for the last time. There were no more excuses to keep seeing them, and he hadn't come and begged her to stay in his life. She'd done her job and she wasn't needed any more.

As she pulled away it occurred to her she really needed to wash her windscreen. She could hardly see where she was going when her vision was so misted up.

'Tell me why you're really here, Ciara.' Cameron waited until Thomas had gone to collect his things before he asked the question which had been burning inside him since her unexpected reappearance in their lives tonight.

'Er...you invited me.' She still had the same smile plastered on her face as she had when she'd first come in. As though it was perfectly normal for her to swan in after three years away and pretend to be part of this family.

'Thomas invited you, but I didn't think

you'd actually show up. It's not as if you've responded to any of my other texts over the past three years. I didn't even know if you'd changed your number.' In those first months after she'd gone he'd sent a flurry of texts asking if she was all right, what he'd done wrong, and if she'd give him a chance to fix things. When her only reply had been a voice message to tell him she was serving him divorce papers, he'd subsequently only contacted her to notify her of Thomas's milestones—photographs of his first day of school every term, losing his first tooth, and the time he'd won a medal on sports day. None of them had prompted her to show any interest in their son's progress so he'd stopped. Until Thomas had asked him to show her the project he'd done. It had meant a lot to him that he shared some of his mother's qualities and Cameron hadn't had the heart to refuse. He was simply surprised it had brought her here tonight.

The smile faltered. 'I needed time... I needed space... I...'

'Did it ever occur to you that Thomas needed you?' He hated that she'd shown up like this without a word. At least if she'd let him know she was coming he could've prepared Thomas, and himself, for seeing her again. This wasn't the ideal place to have this conversation and as much as he wanted to run after Jessie, it wouldn't look good to leave now. He was angry with Ciara, but if there was a chance for her to reconnect with Thomas he had to let it happen. There might never be another opportunity to discuss what had happened and, as with Jessie, he knew there was stuff they hadn't dealt with. If they were ever to have closure they needed to actually talk about what had gone wrong between them.

One thing he'd learned from Jessie was the importance of communication. If he'd been better at it he might never have lost her, and though there was no chance of a reconciliation with Ciara he wanted to understand why she'd left. It might help Thomas if he was able to explain, without guilt or recriminations, what had ended their relationship. He didn't want him going through life the way his father had done, convinced he was the reason loved ones didn't stick around.

Cameron understood it was better for his son to have two parents in his life who would support him. If that was why Ciara was here. He also had to be certain she wasn't going to get their hopes up, only to walk away again when things got too tough.

'Stop with the guilt trip, Cameron. This isn't all on me, you know. Where were you when I needed you? I was depressed and anxious all the time but you were so focused on Thomas you didn't see it.'

'I… I…' He had to think hard about her behaviour before she'd left them. He'd assumed she was being distant because she couldn't cope with Thomas's behaviour, or his diagnosis. It hadn't occurred to him that she was suffering herself, that she might have been ill too. 'I'm sorry, Ciara. I let you down.'

'We both made mistakes, Cameron. If I'd been honest with you about how I was feeling, maybe things wouldn't have got on top of me. I should have got help.'

'I'm a doctor, I should've realised…' Looking back, he knew she had struggled after Thomas's birth but he'd done everything he could to share the childcare and be there for his family. He'd thought it was motherhood in general that she had a problem with, not that she might have had postnatal depression. He should've known better, looked for the signs. It was a wonder they'd lasted as long as they had if she'd been suffering for seven years before she'd had enough. He'd failed her, and Thomas, by projecting his experiences onto his son.

After his upbringing, neglected and emotionally abused by his parents, ignored by the education system, he was afraid of getting it wrong with his child too. He'd put all of his energy into being a good father and in the process hadn't been the best husband. Ciara had suffered the consequences and it was time he stopped solely blaming her for the end of their marriage.

'I didn't even realise. I couldn't figure out why I was so unhappy. I thought if I left and started again I could be the person I used to be. It didn't work out like that.'

'So where have you been all this time?'

'I used up a lot of favours with old friends and family, drifted from one menial job to another, and I'm ashamed to say got into some relationships that weren't good for my mental health either.'

The information should have been a dagger to his heart, not least because he'd been so wounded he hadn't even looked at another woman until Jessie came back into his life. Except the only emotion he felt was sadness, for Ciara, and for him, that these past years had been so difficult.

'And now you're back.' He was sure there was a point to all of this, to her turning up out of the blue after three years of silence, and he'd prefer to get to the bottom of it now. If he was ever going to move on, if there was a chance he and Jessie could be together, he needed to know the mistakes he'd made in the past. Not just so he could make amends to Ciara and Thomas, but also so he could be the man Jessie needed him to be. He didn't want to mess up again.

'It's not like I haven't thought about him, or you, over the years. I just thought it would be better to let you get on with things. You were always better with him than I was.'

'That's not…' He let the words trail off

because it was true and there was no point in pretending otherwise. That didn't mean she shouldn't be in Thomas's life. 'There's still time, you know, to be a mother to him.'

'You...you'd let me do that?' The confident Ciara who'd breezed in had been replaced with the uncertain woman she'd been the last time he'd seen her. When Thomas had come along it had seemed as though she'd lost her sense of self. His bubbly, creative wife had taken to shutting herself away, emotionally and physically. As if she'd been trying to block Cameron and Thomas out of her life. Then one day she'd made it permanent.

'It's not about me letting you do it. I would like Thomas to have his mother back in his life, but only if I know you're not going to walk out on him again. We both have to learn to trust you again and that starts with telling me why you're here now.'

He'd been resisting a relationship with Jessie, who he still had feelings for, because he was afraid of him and Thomas getting hurt. It was only natural he'd apply the same rules to another woman who'd abandoned him. That said, if he was thinking about giving Ciara a second chance, he needed to consider extending Jessie the same courtesy. If she would even talk to him again. He had a lot to say to her, some things to explain, and questions to ask. Having Ciara turn up had proved a couple of things to him—that his marriage was definitely over, and he didn't want to lose Jessie.

'I got help. I'm seeing a doctor and a counsellor regularly. It took me a while to settle, to figure out what I wanted in life. I know that came too late after getting married and starting a family, but I didn't realise I'd feel so overwhelmed by it all. Anyway, I've got a good job as a graphic designer in the area, I've got my own apartment, and I've had time to think about things. About how I treated you and Thomas. I was wondering how I could get to know him again when you texted me and I thought this might be the time to get reacquainted with my son.'

Cameron immediately folded his arms, a defence mechanism as he recalled those desolate feelings of rejection and confusion surrounding her sudden abandonment. 'I'm not going to lie, I was devastated when you walked out. It could've been handled differently, but we both made mistakes. I probably should've taken some time to talk things out, to see how Thomas's issues were affecting you too.'

She gave him a watery, grateful smile. 'Thank you for that. In hindsight, I think we got married too young. We should have been mature enough to talk all of this out back then, but we weren't big on communication, were we?'

'I guess not.' He'd never really learned to communicate his feelings well when his parents never wanted to hear anything he had to say. It was easier to keep everything to himself, or so he'd thought. Now he realised it had cost him his marriage. He didn't want to make the same mistakes with Jessie.

'Part of the reason I delayed getting in touch was because I was worried you would hate me. Then you sent me that message and I saw Thomas's work and I just knew I had to see him. I want to be his mother again. I know I'm ready and now I've moved back to the area I can see him all the time.'

'Whoa. Yes, he's doing well, and tonight is a big achievement, but he still has the same struggles with school and expressing himself. Even if you think you're up to dealing with that it's going to take time for him to get to know you again.' He was always going to put Thomas's feelings first and his own weren't as complicated as he'd imagined upon the first meeting with his ex-wife since she'd left him.

At intervals over the years he'd imagined this scenario and how he would react. It varied between begging her to come back in those early days, to a need to vent his hurt and anger at the way she'd simply vanished and left him to pick up the pieces. Seeing her now though, tentatively reaching out to her son and admitting to her mistakes in the past, had given him a certain closure. He wasn't wistful or nostalgic about the life they'd once had together, the way he had been about Jessie, and he certainly didn't feel the need to play the blame game, or to call her out for everything he and Thomas had been through since. It was surprising to find he no longer had strong feelings of any kind towards her. They were reserved for another woman he needed to see before he blew that relationship too.

'I'll have some leave from work soon. I thought perhaps Thomas could stay with me, or we could have a little trip together somewhere. You could come too, if you'd like, and be a proper family again.' She tilted her head to one side and batted her eyelashes at him, but that no longer had the same effect on him it used to. He didn't know exactly what she was hoping to come from this meeting tonight, but he had to make it clear he wasn't part of the deal.

With a shake of his head, he shot down the possibility that they could be together again before it grew out of control. 'That's never going to happen, Ciara. I'm a different person too and, if I'm honest, there's someone else in my life now. I think it's too early for Thomas to stay away overnight, but if he wants to see you and spend time with you, I have no problem with that. We can take things from there.'

'It was worth a try. For us, I mean. But I'm

more than happy if I can spend some time with my son again.'

If she was disappointed or relieved that Cameron wasn't going to be part of the new version of Ciara she didn't show it as Thomas came bounding back.

'Can we go and get milkshakes now?'

'Sure. I think you've earned it.'

'Can Mum come too?'

Two sets of eager eyes landed on him, waiting for an answer.

'If that's what you want, son, Mum can come too.' That would be a good ice-breaker, a short reintroduction which would be easier for Thomas to digest than diving straight into living with a relative stranger. Ciara too would have to get used to being around Thomas. They'd have to take one step at a time and hope for the best.

'What about Jessie? Is she coming?' He peered behind Cameron, apparently expecting to see her in the background. Of course he knew why she'd felt she had to leave, even if she was wrong, but it wouldn't have been fair to deny Thomas this chance with his mother in case it had been lost for ever. He had to hope she would understand.

'Not this time, buddy.'

'Where is she?'

'I...er...she had to go. Something came up but she said to tell you well done.' He cleared his throat to dislodge the lie, not enjoying the crestfallen look he'd put on his son's face.

'Jessie? Is this your "someone else"?' Ciara quizzed, putting him on the spot, and he was grateful when Thomas butted in to save him from trying to explain she was the woman he'd never stopped loving.

'She's a friend of Dad's and mine. It was Jessie's idea to paint for my project. I thought she'd want to go for milkshakes with us.' Thomas pouted.

'Maybe next time.' If she ever agreed to see him again outside of work.

'Uh-huh. She sounds great. Maybe you should see if she wants to join us?' Ciara was reaching out, telling Cameron that she wanted to be part of his and Thomas's life, even if that included befriending a new woman in his life. She wasn't to know he'd been so scarred by their past he'd barely let a potential partner breach his defences. That it had taken his first love reappearing in his life for him to realise he'd never got over losing her.

However, if he didn't act now, tell Jessie how he felt about her, what he wanted for them, he could lose her for ever.

CHAPTER EIGHT

'YOU'RE LATE TONIGHT.'

'I told you I had that school thing with Cameron and his son tonight, Mum. Thomas did really well, he won this awesome cup—' She ended the story there before she came to the part where Cameron's ex turned up and she was suddenly on the outside looking in.

'It's nice that you're spending time together again. Do you think you'll make another go of it?'

'No.' Although she was firm in her denial with her mother, Jessie was still conflicted over the matter. It was clear to her that while she still had feelings for Cameron, and perhaps harboured a fantasy of them being together again, it wasn't going to happen.

With Ciara back on the scene she knew her time was up. Not only had Thomas wanted her there but also Cameron had invited her, and never said a word, leaving Jessie as the intruder in what was clearly a family moment, celebrating their son's achievement. She was nothing more than an assistant who'd pointed him in the right direction and was now in danger of outstaying her usefulness, along with her welcome.

'That's a shame,' her mother said, eating the pieces of roast chicken and broccoli Jessie had cooked for her earlier.

The doorbell rang, likely one of her mother's carers to help get her into bed. At least with company in the house she mightn't be tempted to wallow too much in her self-pity.

'I'll get it. You finish your dinner.' Jessie sighed out her misfortune in a deep, long breath as she opened the door. Only to forget how to breathe altogether when she saw who was standing on her doorstep.

'Cameron? What are you doing here? Where's Thomas?' She glanced behind him, but there didn't appear to be anyone else with him.

'He's with his mother, having a milkshake. I don't want to leave him for too long, but I needed to see you. To explain.'

'You don't need to explain anything. Ciara's back. It's what you all want—need. Thomas's project is finished so there's no reason for me to keep tagging along.' She was clutching the door, keeping it as a barrier between her and Cameron in an effort to protect what was left of her shattered heart.

'Ciara might be back but we're not together, and we're not going to be. There's only one woman I'm interested in.' He took a step through the door, forcing Jessie to let him inside, her heart hammering with the anticipation of what he was going to say.

'Oh?' She didn't dare to believe he was talking about her until he actually said the words.

'You,' he said without further hesitation, gathering her in his arms for a swoon-worthy kiss, sealing how he felt about her once and for all.

'But…but what about Ciara and Thomas? How are we going to do this without upsetting anyone?' There was no question that she wanted to be with him, and pretending otherwise hadn't worked out, but those obstacles preventing their happy ending were still there on the horizon, casting a shadow over her potential jubilation.

'I've made it clear to Ciara that we aren't getting back together, but she's welcome to see Thomas. Although I think she'd already figured out my heart was with some one else.' He was looking down at her, his eyes filled with so much love for her, Jessie was afraid to leave his embrace to join the real world and have this moment of feeling wanted and loved completely disappear.

'I'm scared, Cameron.' Of getting hurt, of him not loving her as much as she loved him, but most of all of losing him again.

'Me too.' He grinned. 'But Ciara coming back has made me take a good hard look at myself. I wasn't there for her and our marriage ended because we weren't honest with each other about our feelings. I lost you for the same reason. So I'm putting it all out there now. I still love you and it frightens the life out of me, but it's clear I can't be without you any more.'

'Jessie, who's at the door?' Right on cue,

her mother hollered from the living room and ruined the moment. Just when all of her dreams were coming true she was reminded that she had responsibilities to keep her from floating away on the fantasy.

'It's me, Mrs Rea, Cameron Holmes,' he yelled back, and Jessie found herself giggling at the untimely interruption.

'Come in so I can see you,' she demanded.

Jessie reluctantly let go of him and led him into the lounge, standing awkwardly as though she was introducing her first boyfriend. Which, she supposed, he still was.

'Hmm, you've filled out a bit from the last time I saw you. Good, that means you can help this one get me to bed.'

'Mum! Cameron hasn't come here to nursemaid you.'

'He's a doctor, isn't he? I'm sure he can help me get to my feet at least.' Ignoring Jessie's protests, her mother pushed her half-eaten dinner aside and beckoned Cameron.

'It's good to see you, Mrs Rea.' Ever the gentleman, Cameron offered her his arm so she could lever herself out of the armchair.

'You too. I always thought you two made a good couple.'

'Mum.' Exasperated by her mother's matchmaking, Jessie took her other arm so they could get her to bed in double-quick time.

Her mother's makeshift bedroom was in the former dining room, a change they'd made when she could no longer manage the stairs. Now it was filled with her mother's personal possessions and a mechanical bed.

Her mother stopped to peer closely into Cameron's face. 'She always loved you, you know. That's why she sent you away. She didn't want to hurt you.'

'Cameron has to go and pick his son up now, and I'm sure you're very tired, Mother.' Jessie glared at her, silently begging her not to say anything else. They were only just getting to know one another again and she didn't want to ruin things by raking up the past again.

Thankfully, her mother said nothing more on the subject and let them help her into bed.

'I'm so sorry about Mum. She shouldn't have said anything.' Jessie waited until she was seeing Cameron out at the door before she said anything more.

'It's all right. I'm glad you had someone to talk to and didn't go through it alone. How is she these days?'

'She has carers who come in three times a day to help her get washed and make her meals, but it's not unheard-of for her to send them away, insisting she can manage herself. She can't, of course. The stroke made an independent life impossible.'

Cameron opened the front door but turned around to face her before he set foot outside again, as though he'd been thinking about every word she'd uttered.

'So she relies on you to pick up the slack. That doesn't seem very fair on you.'

'She doesn't have anyone else. Neither do I.'

Cameron took her face in his hands and held her so close she could feel his breath on her skin. 'You have me. I want to be with you, Jessie. I don't know how we're going to manage it, or what will happen, but I'm sure of that.'

When he said it like that she was convinced every word was true. They'd take things one step at a time and, for now, being with him was enough.

'You should get back to Thomas. Thanks for coming to see me.' She appreciated that he'd left his family to come and clarify things with her but she didn't want it to come at the expense of Thomas's welfare. They were both going to have to learn to give and take when it came to each other's time and loyalties so they could be together.

'You're important to me. Remember that.' He dropped a kiss on her lips, so sweet and tender she could still feel it even after he'd got into his car.

'I hope you're not having second thoughts.' Cameron was waiting for her outside the main entrance to the hospital, their agreed meeting place for their first date since she couldn't face having to deal with her mother's input on the matter.

'Of course not. I was just checking on Simon. He was having some pain in his knees during our session so I thought I'd give him a joint rub to try and ease things for a bit.'

'Is there anything I can do?' The joyful smile he'd been wearing to greet her crinkled into a frown at the prospect of their favourite patient suffering any more than he already had.

'I think it's just from exercising the joints again. He's working hard and making great progress. If it gets any worse I'll let you know.' She didn't think it was anything more serious than overuse of the limbs that had been immobile for a while and were now getting used to being put through their paces again. If it didn't improve, Cameron would be her first port of call to investigate in case there were any complications they hadn't foreseen.

'Good. I know I'm not here as much as usual but you know I'll do whatever I can for him. Any progress on the search for family?'

'Not yet. Once he's well enough to leave the ward he'll have to go into foster care. Not a great incentive for him to get better but there doesn't seem to be an alternative.'

Now that Simon was well on his way to

recovery there was no reason for Cameron to be here all the time any more, other than for the odd check-up. He still quizzed Jessie after her physiotherapy sessions with him but their time together was limited these days. They'd managed to snatch the odd kiss when they'd crossed paths but it hadn't been enough for either of them so they'd agreed to make time for a proper date, a big step for both of them.

He kissed her on the cheek before opening the car door for her. That graze of his skin against hers, the feel of him, was enough to give her pulse, and her mood, a lovely lift. She'd been looking forward to seeing him all day and this was her reward after dealing with difficult poorly patients.

'So, where are we going?' she asked, little bubbles of excitement fizzing in her veins for the night ahead when he'd kept it all secret from her this far.

'I'm not telling you until we get there,' he teased. 'You look beautiful, by the way.'

The unexpected compliment made her sit taller in the passenger seat, pleased with herself for making an effort even though he'd told her just to wear something casual. A date with Cameron was never going to be something she took for granted so she'd taken some time after her shift to do her make-up and shake her hair loose from its ponytail confines. One quick change from her uniform into some silky black trousers and a dusky rose wrap-over blouse and she was date-ready. She could get used to this double life, swapping wheelchairs and ice packs for mystery dates with a handsome man every night.

'Thank you. You're not so bad yourself.' She winked at him in the rear-view mirror, delighted by his bashful blush at the returned compliment. Even if he didn't realise, he was a very attractive man. Tonight he'd dressed in black jeans and a mossy green T-shirt, an outfit which usually wouldn't draw attention, except on him the slim fit emphasised the lean body barely contained within. Casual but still gorgeous.

'Ciara's taking Thomas for something to eat then on to the cinema, so we're not in any rush to get back,' he said, as though trying to deflect her obvious ogling.

'It's good they're getting on.' Although she would probably always hold some residual resentment, along with some envy, of the woman who'd given Cameron a family, Jessie admired her for having the courage to come back and build some bridges. It was better for a child to have two parents who loved him and wanted the best for him. And having someone else to share the childcare with would hopefully give them some quality time together in the future.

'Ciara's eager to catch up on everything Thomas is doing and so far he's enjoying sharing his sketches and getting to know her again. I think it's been good for all of us to have her back and work through our family issues. They're planning a trip to an art museum soon so we could maybe earmark that for our second official date.'

'I'd like that.' Although it was strange for her to think Cameron's ex was on the scene, Jessie knew it was helping him and Thomas deal with the past. He was much more open about his feelings now and she was doing her best to do the same to avoid making the same mistakes as before.

They were all entering into these newly forged relationships with caution in an effort to prevent anyone from getting hurt, and with good reason. All of them were nursing old war wounds but were determined to move on to a happier shared future.

Cameron reached across and squeezed her hand, holding it until they came to their final destination.

'I thought it was about time you experienced your first funfair.'

It didn't matter that it wasn't the place the cool kids once hung out, or that she was older than the teens rushing through the turnstile, eager to get right into the middle of the fun, Jessie was elated as Cameron made her dreams come true. It was so thoughtful of him to bring her somewhere she'd never got to experience as a child because she'd had to look after her mother. It was such a considerate place to take her on their first date that she couldn't stop herself flinging her arms around his waist and hugging him so hard she'd probably left an imprint of her face on his chest.

'Thank you.'

'If I'd known I'd get this reaction I would have brought you here a long time ago.'

'I wish you had.' Regardless of her high spirits, a dagger of regret would remain embedded in her heart for ever that they'd spent all of these years apart, hurting.

Cameron squeezed her back. 'Hey, no looking back, okay? Only forward from now on.'

He was right. The past held only painful memories of struggle and loss, when the future currently seemed as bright as the flashing neon lights beckoning them deeper into the carnival atmosphere. Here, now, with Cameron and the night ahead, she had so much to look forward to.

'I want to do everything, okay?' She took in the rides, the food stalls, the games, and she wanted to be part of it all. Reliving the childhood she'd never got to have, with Cameron, the only man she'd ever wanted to experience it with.

'Fine by me.' He paid for armbands which gave them unlimited access to the rides, but Jessie's first stop was at the concession stand.

'A candyfloss, please.'

Cameron insisted on paying, even though he didn't get himself anything. Jessie pulled off a chunk of fluffy spun sugar from the stick and let it settle on her tongue, coating it in sticky sweet joy.

'This is so good,' she said, sticking her face into the pink cloud to bite off another chunk.

'You're enjoying that, huh?' Cameron picked tufts of excess candyfloss from her hair and her cheek with a grin.

'You need to taste this.' She plucked a piece off and shoved it into his mouth.

'It's very sweet.' He laughed, licking the sugary substance from his lips.

Jessie was overcome with the need to kiss him, so she did, revelling in the sweet, warm, moreish taste of him on her tongue.

'Let's start with those spinning things.' She pointed to what looked like a giant mechanical spider with cars attached to each leg.

'Are you sure?' Cameron grimaced as they watched it in action, the cars spinning around as the mechanical legs shot in and out at high speed.

'Chicken?'

'No, too old to get spun around like a whirling dervish.'

'Nonsense, we're still young at heart.' She refused to believe that it was too late to recapture everything she'd missed out on when she was younger, including the relationship she'd hoped to have with Cameron. Life might have passed her by while she'd been busy caring for her mum, but she was seizing it now with both hands.

Cameron followed her over to the ride, protesting all the way. 'I'm serious. I think your centre of gravity changes as you get older and makes you less able to handle things like this.'

They got into the car and clicked the safety bar into place. 'If this is your way of telling me you'll be screaming like a terrified five-year-old I won't think any less of you.'

Cameron didn't get the chance to deny the charges set against him as the ride set in motion, the music and flashing lights increasing in tempo along with the momentum of the machine. It wasn't long before Jessie was the one doing the screaming, the motion and speed taking her breath away with excitement. The twirling, spinning movement of their carriage had her sliding along the double seat until Cameron put his arm around her to anchor her in one place. She was grateful for his steadying hand on her waist, knowing he would keep her safe no matter what.

'I might need some time out before we attempt another one of those,' Cameron joked as he helped her out of her seat. Jessie's legs were wibbly-wobbly as she attempted to step back onto solid ground so she was glad when he took her over towards the carnival stalls instead of veering towards the nosebleed-inducing vertical drop ride nearby.

'At least I can tick that off my list.' She wasn't sure she would do it again but she was over the moon to have experienced her first fairground ride with the boy of her dreams.

The night got even better as he tested his skill at the shooting range, his steady hands and sharp eye earning him enough points for the large stuffed unicorn toy she'd had her eye on.

'Am I getting Brownie points for my first date originality? It's been a while since I had to impress a lady. Although it's made easier by the fact you're that lady, and I know you so well.' His eagerness to please her was just as endearing as him holding her hand as they strolled through the fair like any other young lovers.

For once, Jessie didn't feel the stress of her responsibilities haunting her every move, enjoying living in the moment, free to express her emotions instead of pretending she didn't have them. Of course all their problems weren't solved by one carefree date, but it was a step closer to the life she wanted, the one she should have had all along with Cameron in it.

'It's been a dream come true, thank you,' she said, clutching him with one hand and her cuddly unicorn in the other. 'But yeah, let's take a break before our next bone-shaking ride.'

Soaking up the excitable atmosphere, they

made their way around the fair until they ended up at the hot food wagon.

'Do you fancy sharing some French fries? I suppose as it's a date I should have bought you dinner but I was worried about the effect of going on to a rollercoaster afterwards.'

'I am hungry, and I suppose some fries would be nice…' She was wondering how to break it to him she'd already had her fill of fairground rides without losing face. There was much more fun to be had simply by being in Cameron's company without worrying about anyone else for a little while.

They ordered their food and ate it standing at a nearby upturned beer barrel which had been repurposed into a table. It was such a simple unpretentious meal in less than salubrious surroundings but Jessie knew she would always remember it as one of the best dinner dates she'd ever had.

As Cameron tossed their wrapper into the bin he sniffed the air. 'Can you smell something burning?'

The moment he said it there was a loud bang and she felt an intense heat filling the air. Before she could even figure out what was happening, Cameron had grabbed her arm and pulled her away from the source. When she glanced over her shoulder she saw flames blazing in the hot food van they'd just left, screams emanating from within and the woman who'd served them falling out of the door onto the ground, her clothes and hair on fire.

While other fair-goers looked on in horror, frozen by fear, Jessie and Cameron swung into action. She rolled the woman on the ground, attempting to put out the flames, then was straight onto her phone calling the emergency services as he grabbed the fire extinguisher propped up against the door of the food van. He blasted the extinguisher on to the fire blazing away in the fryer. In a cloud of smoke and steam, he fought until the flames were out and returned to tend to the injured woman outside. He was a real-life action hero, but she was relieved when he emerged again, covered in soot and sweat.

'The paramedics are on their way. So are the fire brigade. I didn't know you were a part-time fire-fighter too.' While Cameron had been battling the source of the blaze, Jessie had loosened the top buttons on the woman's shirt so she could breathe a little easier.

'When you have a ten-year-old son, you're prepared for almost anything,' he countered before coming to rejoin them on the ground.

'My name is Cameron and I'm a doctor. I know you've had a big shock and you're probably in a lot of pain...' he checked the name on her badge '... Debbie, but we need to move quickly to prevent the burn from getting any more serious.'

It was Debbie's right arm and hand that had been badly burned, the remains of her charred sleeve clinging to her reddening skin.

'Jessie is going to remove your jewellery in case there's any swelling, and give it to the paramedics when they get here for safe-keeping.' He gave Jessie the nod to gently slip off the bracelets from her arm, which she did, trying her best not to press against her burned skin. It was necessary to do it now before her injuries became swollen, preventing removal and potentially affecting her circulation.

Someone—likely a carnival worker—had set a first aid box and a blanket beside them. Cameron covered the injured woman with the blanket, careful to avoid the burned areas.

'We need to keep you warm and raise your legs to prevent shock setting in.' He grabbed Jessie's unicorn and used it as a makeshift platform to rest Debbie's feet on.

Debbie was sobbing now, the pain and shock of what had happened beginning to set in.

'The ambulance will be here soon,' Jessie assured her. 'They'll be able to give you something for the pain.'

'Debbie, I'm going to wrap your fingers individually to stop them fusing together. I'll be as gentle as I can.' Using the sterile bandages, he carefully dressed each finger before doing the same for the rest of her arm, covering the area with a loose sterile bandage.

She felt for Debbie, enduring that contact on her burned skin, but she also admired

Cameron's sensitive treatment of her wounds. He was good in a crisis and, yet again, she was reminded that he would have been there for her during her struggles for all this time if she'd let him. She just wished she hadn't wasted so much time apart from him.

CHAPTER NINE

'IT'S NOT QUITE how I saw our date going…'
Cameron pulled up outside his house, aware
that they hadn't spoken since they'd called
an end to the night once the ambulance had
taken Debbie to the hospital. He was worried
that all of the drama had proved too much
during what was supposed to have been their
carefree evening recapturing their youth. If
anything, his job meant he had more responsibility than ever, and not just to his patients,
as events had proved. He hoped it wouldn't
spoil what they were just beginning.

Having Jessie back in his life enriched
it on so many levels. Far beyond how good
she was with Thomas, how extraordinarily
patient and loyal she was to her mother, she
was simply the part of him which had been
missing for all of these years.

They'd been having fun up until the fire, and when they'd been treating the injured woman Jessie had jumped right in there with him. He'd been on his own for so long, doing everything himself, he'd forgotten what it was like to have someone there by his side. It would be devastating to have to go back to that lonely life when he was just realising how much he'd been missing the company, the fun and the love that Jessie brought with her.

They'd been dancing around each other for too long, trying to pretend they didn't need one another, but now he wasn't sure he knew how to be without her. And if he was being honest, he didn't want to be.

'I know, but I enjoyed it. It's a pity it has to end.' Jessie echoed his thoughts and he was reinvigorated at the thought of being given a second chance.

'We still have some time before Thomas gets back. Let me get showered and changed and maybe we can go for a drink or something.' Eager to get the night back on track, he bounded out of the car and let them into the house.

'We don't have to go out. You know, we could totally just veg out here on the couch. I don't mind where we are, Cameron, as long as I'm with you.' Jessie was standing toe to toe with him in the hallway, making it clear to him she wasn't going anywhere. It was sufficient to cause the last vestiges of his restraint to turn to dust.

All night he'd been entranced by her excitement and the way she'd thrown herself into everything, seizing the moment. Now it was his turn.

He caught her around the waist and pulled her towards him, claiming her mouth with his. She tasted sweet and salty, of candyfloss and fries, and everything he craved. Tonight, free from the worries of their everyday lives, they'd been free to be themselves, to be the couple they'd never got to be. He wasn't ready for it to be over yet either.

'Let me go get cleaned up, then I'm all yours.' He wanted to wash off the drama and responsibility again and be the fun person she'd started the night with, to be the best version of him for Jessie.

'You know, I could do with a shower my-

self…' Her eyes, full of mischief and desire, never left his as she began to strip off
her blouse, sending a direct message to his
groin.

'Are you sure?' He watched her undress,
growing increasingly uncomfortable in the
confines of his own clothes, but he didn't
want to rush her into anything. They'd been
taking things slowly and, as much as he
wanted to take it to the next level with Jessie, he didn't want her to regret anything
when she was still wary about getting into
anything serious. She was always conscious
of her mother's needs before her own, but
he was doing his best to accommodate her
duty as a carer along with them having some
quality time together.

She let her blouse fall to the floor and
undid her bra, exposing her full creamy-
white breasts to his gaze and making his
mouth water. 'I'm sure.'

Her determination to show him she was
ready was a strong aphrodisiac, not that he
needed one. When he saw her confidence
waver as she bit her lip, waiting for him to
respond, he went to her quickly. He cupped

her breast, lifted it to his mouth and sucked on the rosy peak until she gasped. One of the good things about knowing her so well was that he was aware of what she liked, what turned her on, and what drove her crazy.

He flicked the pert tip with his tongue, at the same time caressing her other breast and tugging the nipple between his fingers, revelling in her breathy moans of delight, all the time making himself harder than granite. Jessie still made him feel like that horny teenage boy who couldn't get enough of her.

When she felt his erection through his jeans he damn near finished it all too soon. They needed to slow things down, take the time they'd never really had to enjoy one another.

With her face cradled in his hands now he kissed her on the lips, their bodies pressed tantalisingly close, but still not close enough.

'Let's go upstairs,' he whispered into her ear and watched the goosebumps appear on her skin, reflecting his own anticipation for the rest of their evening together.

She took his hand and they moved quickly up the stairs, Cameron shedding his clothes as they went, making Jessie giggle. When they reached the bathroom they were both wearing only their underwear, a problem he solved quickly, divesting Jessie of hers before removing his own.

He reached in to turn on the shower and pulled Jessie into the cubicle with him as he shut the door. Cameron watched the water cascade down the slope of her breasts, her nipples still standing proud and begging for attention. He caught them between his fingers and thumbs, pinching until they were bullet-hard, just like him.

Jessie wound her arms around his neck and pulled him under the stream of water with her as she latched her mouth to his. Her demanding kiss and her need to have him was sexy, intoxicating. He lifted her leg and positioned himself between her thighs, pressing his hardness against her soft mound. She groaned and pushed her body closer until her breasts were squashed against his chest.

He laughed, her sense of urgency a boost to his ego and his libido. After the last three years of thinking only about his son's well-being and locking his own needs away in that empty half of his closet, it felt good to be wanted. Jessie had opened up that part of his life again, that part of being a man, and reminded him that he deserved to be loved too.

'I think we've wasted too much time already. I've decided we need to live in the moment.'

'Uh-huh? You've decided?' he teased, though he loved the sentiment, knowing they were both thinking along the same lines.

'Yeah,' Jessie countered, chin tilted up into the air.

'As sexy as you are wet, I want to wait to take this to the bedroom. I don't want our first time to be over too quick, or end up in the emergency department at the hospital. It's not easy getting purchase on a wet floor in my bare feet and I want to give you one hundred per cent.' He set to work with the shower gel, lathering it over himself first to wash away the remnants of their earlier drama, then taking his time with Jessie. Her breasts were slick beneath his hands, full and heavy in his palms.

'I will take you any way I can have you,'

she teased, nibbling on his earlobe and almost convincing him to stay put.

With an amazing amount of effort he let her go and focused on washing her hair, letting the suds cascade down her delectable body. It was only when she began to return the favour that Cameron's resolve faltered. Her fingers massaging his scalp felt so good, calling to other parts of his body to stand to attention, wanting the same treatment.

He took her by the hand and led her into his bedroom. Standing there naked, her wet hair clinging to her now make-up-free face, she'd never looked so beautiful. She was softer, curvier and sexier than he remembered and he was going to enjoy getting to know her all over again.

The sexiness of their tryst was making Jessie's skin tingle with excitement. Especially when he seemed eager to make it so incredible. He slowed things right down, pulling her back into his arms to kiss her, taking a leisurely possession of her lips that made her weak at the knees. She was thankful when he backed her over to the bed and laid her down. Instead of joining her, he knelt on the floor, moving between her legs so they were resting over his shoulders. When he grinned at her and she realised his intention her eyes just about rolled back in her head in anticipation of the pleasure she knew was coming.

He kissed his way along her inner thigh, the touch of his lips burning her skin, followed by the soothing lap of his tongue. She lay back as arousal took control of her body, giving herself over to Cameron when he parted her with the tip of his tongue. That full feeling of having him inside her was nearly matched by the sensation of him circling that sensitive nub he found easily.

She drifted off on a cloud of bliss, her worries and responsibilities tiny specks in the distance. Only Cameron had the ability to take her mind off every little thing constantly taking up space in her brain, leaving her free to enjoy all the things he was doing to her, making her feel.

When Cameron sucked on that sensitive part of her which seemed to be totally controlling her whole body at present, that floating sensation suddenly changed to something more intense as she spiralled back down to earth, her complete focus on her impending climax at the tip of Cameron's tongue.

She bucked off the bed as her orgasm hit, yet he didn't relent in his pursuit. Jessie called out again and again as he brought her to that peak repeatedly, until she had nothing left to give.

Satiated, content, her body limp after her exertions, she could barely lift her head when he did finally join her on the bed, a condom at the ready.

'Okay?' he asked, dropping a tender kiss onto her mouth.

'More than okay.' She stretched and purred, well and truly satisfied by his attentions.

'I aim to please.' He grinned against her lips, making her smile even more.

'You definitely did that, but what can I say, I'm greedy for more.' With their wet bodies pressed so close together she was already aching for him again.

She reached down and took hold of him, revelling in his breathy gasp. With slow, deliberate movements she moved her hand up and down his shaft, driving them both crazy with desire.

Sex hadn't been a big deal in her life since he'd gone. It had been something she could take or leave with little time to explore a physical or emotional relationship. But she couldn't get enough of Cameron. The first time they'd slept together as naïve teens had lit that spark, that sensation of their bodies joining together quickly becoming addictive. Over the years she'd blamed that sexual awakening for convincing her she was in love, and that a husband and family could be in her future. Now she understood it was only Cameron who elicited those feelings because he was the only man she'd ever truly loved. Making love to him was just that because she'd never stopped loving him. She was afraid to look too far into the future in case her perfect world crumbled down around her again, but for now she was more than happy to live in the moment with him.

He covered her body with his, kissing her neck and beyond until he came to that erogenous zone right behind her ear. As she gasped, shivers tracing his path along her skin where he'd touched her, Cameron thrust inside her. It took a moment for her to adjust, to accept him again after so long. He hesitated too, resting his forehead against hers for a few seconds, his breath unsteady.

'It's been a while,' he confessed, seemingly fighting for control over his impulses.

Jessie stroked the side of his face. 'I know. For me too. There's no pressure. I just want to be with you.'

'Me too. I love you, Jessie. I always have.'

'I love you too.'

The admission of their feelings for one another after so long trying to hide them seemed to break the last of their defences, leaving the way clear for them to fully embrace this time they had together. Jessie opened up to him, taking everything he had to offer as he plunged deep inside her, determined to show the strength of his devotion.

Cameron's panting breath in her ear became a victorious roar drowning out her cry of ecstasy as they rode to that ultimate release together. Their bodies continued to rock, chest to chest, hips to hips, groin to groin, the ripples of their climax reverberating.

'Did you mean what you said?' Jessie asked once she was capable of speech again. She wanted to be sure that his declaration wasn't a crumb tossed her way when he was carried away at the height of their passion. Now that she'd opened her heart for him again she was vulnerable, and afraid another blow would prove fatal.

'I meant every word. I love you, Jessie. I'll get it tattooed if that's what it takes for you to believe me.' He disposed of the condom and came back to lie beside her again, his eyes locked onto hers, beseeching her to believe him.

'I don't think we need to go that far but, you know, maybe a full-page ad in the newspaper would suffice.'

It was easy to joke about it when she believed him, but she was worried that the day would come when it wouldn't be enough. At some point the world outside was waiting to gatecrash their party for two and force them apart.

'I'll book a plane to sky-write it too, just to be sure.'

She felt his chest rise and fall beneath her head as he laughed at his own joke. They were so comfortable together she wished they could stay here for ever, but all too soon the spectre of their responsibilities haunted the perfect moment.

'I should really get back to Mum, and I'm sure Thomas will be on his way soon.'

Cameron groaned. 'I love my son but I wish we could freeze time for a little while longer.'

'I know.' She traced her finger around his nipple, watching with interest as it puckered beneath her touch.

Cameron grabbed her hand. 'If you keep doing that we're going to get in real trouble,' he growled.

Undeterred, Jessie continued her perusal, only for Cameron to flip her over on to her back and straddle her.

'You're such a bad influence,' he said, pinning her hands above her head so she was fully exposed to him. He copied her actions, only this time using his tongue to tease her nipples into the same hard peaks as his.

She bit her lip, trying to resist giving him the satisfaction of hearing her excited moans. When she didn't respond he sucked her nipple hard enough it grazed the roof of his mouth, watching her all the while for a response. She tilted her chin up in silent defiance, only for him to dip a hand between her legs and feel her arousal for himself. He couldn't keep the grin from his face as he reached for another condom from the drawer. And when he forged their bodies together again with a thrust of his hips there was no point in trying to pretend she wasn't in raptures when her body betrayed her so easily.

She clung to him now, the bedroom echoing her cries of ecstasy as Cameron rushed her quick return to oblivion. If only she had him permanently in her life she might never have to think about anything beyond the bedroom ever again.

Their lovemaking this time was frantic, pure lust and the knowledge that their time together was coming to an end driving the need for one last release. Cameron pounded against her until they were both satisfied and exhausted, their bodies slick with sweat.

'I think I'm gonna need another shower,' he gasped between his ragged breaths.

'I'll let you have that one alone or else we'll never get out of here.' Jessie got up, leaving him to recover on top of the bed.

'Sounds good to me,' he said and smacked her backside with his hand.

That kind of sexual possessiveness on her anatomy from a man would usually earn him a slap back, but she liked that he couldn't get enough of her, that he was claiming her as his. She wanted to belong to Cameron as much as she wanted him to be exclusively hers. In her past relationships she'd always remained wary, her fear usually coming true that her partner would grow tired of her commitments elsewhere. With Cameron, she'd gone all in, giving him her body and soul, trusting him not to abuse either. She'd had a wobble in confidence with Ciara back on the scene, but he'd proved to her tonight it was her he would rather be with. Her heart should remain intact for as long as that remained true.

'You need to get dressed too.' She tossed his clothes at him once she'd located hers and put them on.

'Spoilsport.'

'I think I've been sporting enough. Now we need to get back to adulting.' More was the pity.

They drove back to her house in silence, but every now and then Cameron took her hand and placed it on his leg so he could feel her there. She leaned her head against his arm, the occasional sigh of contentment slipping out making him smile.

When they reached their destination, and the end of their wonderful night, Cameron walked her to the front door.

'Thank you for a most enjoyable date,' he said, lifting her hand to his mouth for a kiss, that twinkle in his eye as glittery as Jessie's whole body felt where he'd touched her.

'I don't usually put out on a first date. You're the exception.'

'Very privileged, although I think you'll

find it's our second first date so your reputation is still intact.'

'I think my reputation is in tatters after what we've just done, but it was worth it.' She stood up on her tiptoes to give him a peck on the lips but Cameron had other ideas, wrapping his arm around her and pulling her flush to him. His mouth was crushed against hers, his tongue urgently seeking hers out, as though they were never going to see one another again and this was to be their final kiss. It was hot and intense, full of everything they'd done and wanted to do to each other again in the bedroom.

'Jessie! I need help!' Her mother's urgent cries ripped them apart.

'Mum? What's wrong? I'm coming!' She abandoned Cameron on the doorstep to run towards the bedroom, but she heard his footsteps following her down the hallway and was grateful she'd have him with her to face whatever was behind the door.

When she found her mother lying on the floor, blood pouring from the gash on her forehead, Jessie was overwhelmed by a sense of guilt.

'How long have you been lying here?'

'I don't know,' her mother said weakly. She was very pale, making the scarlet stain spreading over the floor and her white nightgown all the more alarming.

'What happened?' She grabbed a handful of tissues from the box on the nightstand and attempted to stem the bleeding.

'I don't know. I think I got up to make myself a cup of tea and I must have fallen over.'

'I think you must have banged your head on the chest of drawers when you fell, Mrs Rea.' Cameron pointed out the blood staining the white melamine furniture.

'Oh, Mum, I'm sorry I wasn't here for you.' She just about managed to hold back the tears, but she was plagued by images of her and Cameron enjoying their time together as though they didn't have a care in the world.

'I called you,' her mother said, her eyes fluttering shut.

'I'm sorry I didn't answer. Please stay awake.' If anything happened she would never forgive herself.

'The ambulance is on its way,' Cameron told her as he hung up the phone.

Jessie couldn't help but wonder if this would be her some day. If her condition would leave her helpless, dependent on him, when he had his own responsibilities to think about. It didn't matter how much Jessie loved him, she'd been selfish. Fifteen years ago she'd made the most difficult decision of her life because she hadn't wanted to trap him. Yet that was exactly what she was doing now.

Her APS could lead to the same health issues her mother had—strokes, paralysis and a lifelong fear for those around her. It wouldn't be fair on Cameron or Thomas to put them through this in another few years down the line. Her condition had an increased risk of blood clots. That meant a higher chance of developing deep vein thrombosis, strokes, heart attacks or bleeds on the brain. It was one thing asking Cameron to come to terms with not having any more children if he wanted a future with her, but expecting him to give up his life to care for her was selfish. Why would she set him free as a teenager, only to trap him now, except to make herself happy?

She'd spent a life burdened by the guilt of causing her mother pain, she couldn't do it again with Cameron.

'You can go. I'm sure Thomas will be on his way home by now.' She pulled her mother's quilt off the bed and covered her in an effort to keep her body temperature raised.

'I'm not going to leave you—'

'Mum, open your eyes for me, please. You need to stay awake.' With a head injury she needed to keep her mum conscious.

'Please let me help, Jessie,' he pleaded, but she had to do this on her own. If she'd remembered that she might not have been in this position and her mother might not have been hurt in her absence.

'Just go, Cameron.' She sighed, the fight dying inside, along with all of those hopes and plans she'd made with him for a second time. This was exactly why she'd sent him away the first time around; he made her forget the reality of her situation and what it could mean for him. She wasn't a carefree thirty-something who could spend an evening at the funfair or fooling around in bed without consequences. She was a time bomb.

CHAPTER TEN

CAMERON WAS DETERMINED not to let Jessie
push him away again but he had to go back
to collect Thomas before he tried to make
another stand. If it hadn't been such early
days for Ciara back in their lives he would've
asked her to mind him overnight so he could
be with Jessie but he couldn't rush Thomas.
It would take time for his son to build trust
with his mother and he couldn't take advan-
tage of that simply so he could pursue a romantic relationship.

But he knew it had frightened Jessie to
see all that blood. She was close to her mum
and it was natural for her to feel guilty about
being out tonight, missing when she needed
Jessie's help. Even though the same accident could've happened when she'd been at
work or in the house. He felt the same when

it came to Thomas but he knew he had to move past that guilt because he wanted to be with Jessie. She would have to do the same if they were ever going to have a chance of being together.

Hopefully, she would realise she didn't have to do everything on her own, that he would be there for her. If she'd let him, he could share the responsibility and help carve out some time for them.

Looking to the future, he hoped it would make things easier for him and Jessie to spend time together now Ciara was there to share the childcare. He was sure Thomas would enjoy visiting museums and art galleries with his mother, exploring their common passions and getting to know one another again. It would also take time for Ciara to get used to his idiosyncrasies, and learn how to deal with them. Forcing them to spend time together too soon could have repercussions and set back their blossoming relationship if they didn't tread carefully.

Managed carefully, he hoped they could all benefit from Ciara being back, including Jessie.

'Is Jessie's mum going to be all right?' Thomas cut through his introspection as they hurried through the hospital corridor to find the pair Cameron had left behind to get his son.

'I hope so. She had a nasty fall but the paramedics would have taken care of her. I just want to make sure she and Jessie are okay.'

'It's nice to have a mum again. I'd hate it for anything to happen to mine. Jessie must be very upset.'

Cameron ruffled Thomas's hair. He was glad his evening with his mother had gone so well and would hopefully lay the groundwork for future interactions. His son deserved to have two loving parents in his life.

'She is, that's why I want to pop in and see her. Now, you sit here, you can play with my phone, and here's some money for the vending machine if you need something to eat or drink. I'll just be in that cubicle so shout if you need me, I won't be long.' He deposited Thomas in the seat outside the bay he'd been directed to by the receptionist and emptied his pockets to keep his son content while he tried to rescue his burgeoning relationship with the woman he loved.

'Okay, Dad,' Thomas mumbled, his attention already taken by the small screen in his hand.

Cameron walked over to the cubicle, where the curtain was partially opened. Jessie was sitting at her mother's bedside, head hung as though she'd been caught doing something wrong.

'Is it all right if I come in?'

'Cameron? What are you doing here?'

He watched as her emotions crossed her face—initial surprise followed by a smile, which eventually gave way to a frown.

'I wanted to make sure you were both all right. If it hadn't been for Thomas I would've stayed.' He wanted her to know he wasn't going to give up so easily this time and it had simply been circumstances which had got in the way as usual.

'She has a mild concussion so they're keeping her overnight for observation. How did Thomas get on with Ciara?' She was still holding her mother's hand even though the older woman appeared fast asleep and would have no concept of her being there. It wouldn't surprise him if Jessie slept in the seat all night to assuage some of the guilt eating her up over the fact she hadn't been there when her mother had hurt herself.

'Good. I think they're bonding. I'm glad your mother wasn't seriously hurt.' He hovered at the edge of the cubicle, knowing he wasn't welcome but also aware he hadn't done anything wrong except love Jessie.

There was an uneasy atmosphere, a heavy silence between them which seemed to go on for ever, punctuated only by the sound of the medical equipment monitoring her mother's progress.

'Jessie, I—'

'Cameron—'

They spoke over one another then laughed like awkward teenagers.

'You go first,' he insisted.

She glanced down at her clasped hands in her lap before she lifted her eyes to meet his and he knew she was gearing herself up to end things again. Knowing what was coming didn't make it any easier to stomach.

'I'm sorry for the way I spoke to you

back there, but after what's happened to-night it's made it clear we can't keep seeing each other.'

'I don't understand. I know you've had a shock and you feel bad about not being there for your mother, but we were having a good time up until then, weren't we? Don't be hasty about this, Jessie.' He wanted her to think back beyond finding her mother, to the fun they'd had together at the funfair, and later, in bed. It was too special to throw away after one hiccup, which shouldn't even have affected them as a couple. He couldn't wait another fifteen years to be with her because she felt guilty about leaving her mother when the accident could've happened at any time.

Her blush put some much-needed colour in her cheeks again.

'I'm not denying that, but can't you see, this could be me?' She indicated her mother lying helpless on the hospital bed. 'I have nothing to offer but an uncertain future. I've spent my life as a carer, I don't want the same for you. Being with me would be a life sentence for you and Thomas and reliving my childhood or wanting to be with a man isn't going to change that.'

'I'm not just any man, Jessie. I love you, and I know you love me. We can work this out. There's no guarantee your condition will worsen.'

'There's no guarantee it won't.'

Having done his homework on APS, he ignored her stubborn retort. 'You're already taking a low dose of aspirin to lower the chances of blood clots, right? Most people with your condition can lead normal healthy lives, and you've been doing okay so far. I mean, I know you lost the baby but there's still an eighty per cent chance you could carry full-term.'

'I told you I don't want to go through that again. See, you'd be better off with someone else if you are thinking about having more children.'

'I'm not. I just want you to realise your life doesn't have to stop. Don't do this to me—to us—again. You gave up medical school and a future together, making decisions on my behalf. For once, let me have a say in what happens next. There's no reason you can't live a normal life and I want to be part of it.' He moved towards her but Jessie didn't let go of her mother's hand to meet him halfway.

'I'm sorry, Cameron. I've made up my mind. There was a reason I ended things before. I don't want to be the one holding you back. Tonight was fun, a fantasy, but we both know it's not real and it's naïve and selfish to pretend otherwise. Where's Thomas now?'

'He's out in the corridor, why?'

'Because until I came along you would never have dreamed of leaving him out there. By being together we're only neglecting the other people we love. Let's quit before anyone else gets hurt. I need to look after my mother and you should do the same for Thomas. If something happened to him when we were out galivanting I'm sure you'd feel the same.'

He must have hesitated too long, considering that scenario but certain there would always be room for Jessie in his life.

'Anyway, Ciara's back now. I'm sure she would happily jump in to fill that space in the family. You don't need me.' She turned away from him so easily he wondered if she was simply using her mother as an excuse to get rid of him after all.

The thought made his stomach plummet as though he'd been on that dead drop ride they'd seen at the funfair. Cameron had gone against all of his self-preservation instincts to open his heart to Jessie and welcome her into his family, his bed, his life, only for her to drop him again as if none of it mattered.

'I love you, Jessie,' he said softly, not sure she'd even heard when she didn't look at him.

'Dad? I got my hand stuck in the drawer of the vending machine. It really hurts.' Thomas appeared next to him, clutching his red fingers, making Cameron feel like the worst dad in the world for leaving him, just as Jessie had predicted.

'Let's get that under the cold tap. Hopefully it won't need to be X-rayed.' He put an arm around Thomas's shoulder and guided him out of the cubicle, but not before he'd spoken to Jessie.

'Sorry about your mum, Jessie. I hope everything's okay. Mums are the best.'

'Thanks, Thomas,' she said, offering a smile which apparently Cameron didn't deserve.

If her mother and his son weren't here this would've been a very different scene indeed. Instead he had to swallow his emotions, hold back from kissing her senseless and reminding her how good they were together, because it wouldn't have been appropriate in front of their audience. It didn't mean he was giving up on them, even if she was.

Jessie was tempted to hook herself up to her mother's heart monitor to make sure hers was still beating. When Cameron finally turned around and walked away, admitting defeat, she sucked in a long shaky breath, desperate to get some air back in her lungs. She didn't want him to go, to walk out of her life for ever, but she knew it had to be done. They were addicted to one another, to the point of excluding reality. She knew how it was to be a carer, to lose her identity and a life of her own, and would never inflict that on him or Thomas.

It looked as though Ciara was slotting nicely back into the family and he hadn't argued when Jessie had suggested her as a possible replacement. She was Thomas's mother after all and she and Cameron had a longer relationship than they had ever managed. It made sense for them to get back together, even if the thought of it made her want to retch. He was right about one thing, though—she loved him. So much it felt as if part of her was dying by sending him away again, pushing him towards another woman who could give him a future and make him happy.

Cameron shouldn't be punished for loving her—he'd opened up his heart, and his life, to share it with someone again. If it couldn't be her it should be someone else he had a history with, whom he probably still loved deep down.

She would never have a husband or family when no one would live up to Cameron. If she couldn't have a life with him, she didn't want it with anyone.

* * *

'Thanks for being here. I just wanted to up-date you on Simon's situation.' The social worker who had been in charge of the case had asked Cameron for a meeting and he'd courteously invited Jessie to attend.

'Without strings,' he'd assured her over the phone.

She'd been in two minds whether to even answer his call in case it sent her right back into that dark place she'd been trying to crawl out of since they'd broken up, only a week ago. This time around, losing him seemed to hurt so much more. Perhaps it was because they were adults now, with stron-ger emotions, or maybe it was the sense that time was running out for her to have a life of her own, but Jessie had struggled to move on from him this time. When they'd been teen-agers she'd been heartbroken but she'd man-aged to lock away memories of him along with her feelings in order to move on. It wasn't so easy to do this time around. She still wanted him and that life he represented and seeing him again was killing her, but they both wanted what was best for Simon.

'Have any of his family come forward?' she asked, hoping some good news would take her mind off the man sitting across the table from her, who was sporting a few days' beard growth. Despite her attempt to do the right thing by him, the thought that he perhaps hadn't bounced straight back to his ex, and might also be having some problems getting over her, did give her a fluttery feeling in the pit of her stomach.

'I'm afraid not. Unfortunately, his parents don't seem to have had any surviving family members. That's what brings me here today. I can see from the medical reports that Simon is due to be released from hospital soon and he's expected to make a full recovery.' The social worker's pursed lips suggested this wasn't the happy news it seemed.

'So what happens to him now?' Cameron was frowning as he got to the crux of their concerns.

'Simon is going to have to go into the care system. We'll do our best to place him with a suitable foster family as soon as possible.' She shuffled through her case notes as Jessie stared at Cameron in distress. For someone who had already been through so much, putting the boy into care seemed to be merely adding to his woes.

'And this foster family, will there be other children there?' Cameron asked. She knew he was concerned that Simon would get overlooked in a houseful of other troubled children.

'Most likely. Our experienced foster parents usually take on a few of our children in need. We wouldn't want to put him with anyone just new to fostering when he's going to have ongoing needs.'

'Yes, Simon is going to require a lot more hospital visits to complete his rehabilitation. It's important the family understands that.' Jessie too was worried that a family with so much responsibility would find it difficult to find the time for his extra appointments for physiotherapy and check-ups. It wouldn't be the first time she'd had a young patient disappear off the radar when the parents struggled to find the time, or transport, to make their appointments, often considering their child 'cured' once they were back on their feet. In this case, both she and Cameron knew it would be some time before the boy was fully recovered.

'Our foster carers will have all relevant notes on Simon and we will still be checking in on him, don't worry.'

Easier said than done.

'Will the family be local? I hope he won't lose the connections he's made here since he lost his parents. I don't want him to feel alone in the world.' Cameron was unsurprisingly emotional on the matter, no doubt including himself and Jessie on that list of friends Simon had made during his time at the hospital. He was a wonderfully compassionate man. But she knew that, and that was why she loved him. Why she'd had to let him go. He already had his hands full with Thomas and work, he didn't need to take on her and her mother too. Jessie never wanted to inflict extra pressure on Cameron. Even though it hurt like hell.

Seeing him again had simply opened up that raw wound where her heart had once resided. Especially in these circumstances where he'd proved once again what a kind, caring person he was to be so concerned with one patient's welfare. He was a great doctor and father, and she knew he would've been a fantastic partner if they'd ever stood a real chance of being together long-term.

'We'll do our best to house him in the same area, and I promise that we'll look out for him.' She began to pack her files away, although they'd had less than satisfactory answers to their concerns.

'And wherever he goes won't be permanent, I assume?' Jessie had visions of him being transferred from one house to the next, having to adapt to new families and schools with every move.

Agnes, the social worker, stood, her hands braced on the desk, clearly exasperated by their inquisition. 'Look, we want Simon to have a permanent loving family as much as you do and we'll do what we can to ensure that happens.'

'I understand.' Jessie knew it was out of their hands and Cameron would be every bit as upset as she was that it had come to this for Simon. He was just a little boy grieving for his parents and he needed love and stability. It didn't seem a lot to ask for but it was a case of circumstance. Simon didn't get a say in what happened to him.

She was the kind of person always pre-empting the worst in an effort to protect those around her. Her whole childhood had centred around taking care of her mother and making sure she was all right. So her life had been stagnant and unfulfilling through her own choices. The illness she lived with had cost her her baby, but it had been her decision to send Cameron away when the only happiness she'd truly known was with him. If only it had been as simple as loving each other, wanting to be there for one another, she knew nothing would have kept them apart.

'I just thought I should let you know what's happening. I'll keep in touch,' Agnes said before leaving the room.

'We'll still see him at his appointments.' Cameron moved around the table to be with her, offering her some comfort at a time when she was overwhelmed by melancholy for both Simon and herself.

'I suppose… Will you still be working

here then?' When she'd called things off she hadn't factored in that she might have to keep seeing him at work, making it harder than ever to live without him.

'I would like to continue monitoring Simon's recovery, yes. Although if you didn't want our paths to cross I'm sure we could arrange to see him at different times.'

'I'm not sure that's necessary. It wouldn't be very professional.'

'Perhaps not, but you know I would do anything for you, Jessie. If I thought you didn't love me I would walk away and never bother you again. You know I would rather have a future with you, come what may, than be without you. It's you who insists on making the sacrifice.'

He walked out of the office and Jessie was glad he didn't resort to desperate tactics to get her back, like kissing her one last time to show her what she was missing. Because she wasn't sure she would put up a fight.

'I've left you something to eat and drink by the side of your bed here, so there's no need for you to try and get up. I'm just going to pop to the shops to get a few things. I won't be long, then I'll come back and we can watch TV together.' Jessie tucked her mum in bed, making sure she had everything she could possibly need beside her for the few minutes while she was out of the house. The fall had knocked their confidence, showing them how frail and vulnerable she had become lately. She was more dependent on Jessie than ever, leaving no room for any wistful thoughts about the life she could have had with Cameron.

'You really do need to get a life, Jessie.'

'Pardon me?' For the life of her, Jessie couldn't understand why helping her into bed and giving her everything she needed would have prompted that particular comment.

'You're young. You should have more to look forward to after work than getting an old woman into bed or going to the store for groceries.'

Jessie continued plumping her pillows for her. 'I'm looking after you, Mum.'

'But you love *Cameron*.'

The reminder caused a small, sharp stabbing pain in her gut but she powered on through it. 'It doesn't matter. He has his family to look after and I have mine.'

'I heard you, you know. At the hospital. I know he loves you too.'

'Oh, well, that's all in the past now anyway. Do you need anything from the shop?' She fixed the bedcovers again, even though they were perfectly fine, needing something to keep her thoughts occupied lest they strayed too far back towards Cameron.

Unfortunately her mother wasn't ready to let the matter drop. 'He wants to be with you.'

Jessie sighed. 'I told you, it's over. It doesn't matter what either of us wants.'

'You should be with him instead of wasting your life here with me.'

'Mum, he has Thomas, he doesn't need me to look after too.'

Her mother frowned. 'What are you talking about?'

'APS. No offence, but I don't want to ruin his life if I get sick too.'

'But you're fine, you're taking medication. I had the stroke because I was undiagnosed. Yes, I know you missed out on your childhood to take care of me, but this is different. If it came to it, you would have support. Stop using me and APS as an excuse. Cameron wants to be there for you, and you have a chance of happiness together.'

'What about you?' Jessie plonked down on the end of the bed, her legs no longer able to support her as her mother acknowledged the sacrifices she had made to take care of her.

'I want you to look into assisted living facilities for me—'

'No. I won't do that.' It was everything she'd been trying to avoid over the years, devoting her time to her mother's care so she could stay in her own house.

'It's not up to you, Jessie. I've made my decision. There are people who can look after me twenty-four hours a day if I need them. I'll expect you to come and visit, of course, but you need time and space to carve out a life of your own. I've been selfish for too long.' She patted the back of Jessie's hand with her own, the display of warmth and selflessness finally calling those tears forward.

'What will I do without you?' After so many years being a carer, Jessie didn't know who she was supposed to be, away from these four walls.

'I'm not dead, I'll just be moving away. You seemed to be enjoying a certain doctor's company until I had my little accident anyway. He's waited this long for you, I'm sure he'll take you back in a heartbeat.'

'I don't know, Mum…' As much as she would've loved to run off into the sunset with Cameron, she didn't want to have to give it all up again if circumstances changed.

'I let your father go and never fought for him—for us. That's how I ended up on my own. You lost Cameron once, don't make the same mistake again. Go tell him how you really feel, and make the decision about your future together.'

Jessie thought about what he'd said to her earlier about insisting on making sacrifices, which apparently he didn't think necessary. The last time she'd made decisions for him, with the best of intentions, had taken him out of her life for a long time. If she did the same this time it could be for ever. A life without Cameron now seemed unbearable and it was foolish to punish herself that way when he'd offered her one, even knowing the full circumstances surrounding her health.

She kissed her mother on the cheek. It was true, she had been finding excuses to keep him at a distance because she was afraid of loving and losing him. Her whole life had been shaped around the possibility of her mother dying, and protecting her. Even though he'd never asked her to, she realised she'd been doing the same for him, forcing them apart in a vain effort to save them from getting hurt, only to cause them more pain in the process. They loved each other and that was all that should have mattered.

Suddenly she was excited by the possibilities opening up before her. She could only pray it wasn't too late and Cameron still wanted her to be part of his family.

'Thomas, could we have a chat, buddy?' Cameron patted the seat next to him and beckoned his son over from the table where he'd been painting.

'Sure.' He set down his paintbrush and bounded over, landing on the sofa with a thump. 'Is this about Mum?'

'No. Why would you ask that?'

'I just thought she mightn't want to see me any more or something.' Thomas hung his head, obviously still harbouring some abandonment issues from his younger years.

'Not at all. She loves you. I hope you know that.' He waited for Thomas's nod before he continued. 'No, I wanted to talk to you about Jessie.'

'Is she moving in with us? I know you and Mum aren't getting back together so I thought maybe Jessie would be your new girlfriend.'

It broke Cameron's heart that this new family they were hoping to have wasn't going to include Jessie when Thomas liked her so much. He loved her and if it had been down to him she would be moving in and taking her place in the family portrait, but her stubborn sense of duty had won out over love again for her.

'Sorry, bud, I don't think that's going to happen. Jessie has to stay and take care of her mum.'

He understood his son's pouty response when it was exactly how he felt about the situation—petulant and hard done by—not that it would change things. He had to keep going for Thomas, who would always be his priority, and he doubted he'd find another woman who could replace her anyway. Any thoughts of another relationship would be dead in the water the moment he thought of Jessie and what they could have had together.

The doorbell sounded and put an end to the heart-to-heart with his son.

'Thanks for the chat. You can get back to whatever you were painting.'

'I was sketching a picture of next door's dog for Mum. She likes dogs.' Thomas jumped up and ran off to get his box of craft and Cameron loved that he was so accepting about having his mother back in his life. He only wished Jessie was here to see it.

The bell buzzed again.

'I'm coming,' he yelled, wondering who was being so impatient at this time of night.

When he wrenched the door open he felt as though he'd been punched in the gut. 'Jessie?'

'Hey,' she said with a watery smile that completely undid him.

'Come in. Is everything all right? Is your mum okay?'

'Yes, and yes. I just wanted to see you.'

'Why? I thought you'd made your mind up.' Now that he had time to really look at her he could see she'd come out without a coat in the middle of a cold night, and something didn't seem right about the visit.

Without saying another word, Jessie stood up on her tiptoes, wound her arms around his neck and pulled him down for a kiss. He was too gaga over her to resist, taking the opportunity to indulge in the taste of her once more in case it was the last time. Eventually he knew he had to break it off before he lost himself in her again and forgot they were never going to be together.

'You didn't answer my question,' he said

when he got his breath back from the passionate lip lock she'd engaged him in.

'I'm here because I love you, Cameron, and Thomas. I don't want to lose either one of you.'

A flicker of hope sparked to life in Cameron's chest that he could have it all, including Jessie, but it seemed too good to be true. 'What about your mother? Your illness? What's changed?'

There was little point getting his hopes up, for the same issues to still interfere in the future they wanted together. Her mother's fall proved it could all be taken away in an instant if Jessie's conscience got the better of her and she decided her fears should come before everyone else's needs. He couldn't let her do that to Thomas when he was still reeling from the consequences of her last freak-out.

It was understandable that she wanted to take care of everyone, but she took it to extremes. Making decisions on his behalf that only made them both miserable. That rollercoaster of absolute joy and utter devastation was not something he wanted to ride any more. As he'd told her before, he was too old for those games. All he wanted now was a happy settled life with the people he loved.

'We had a chat tonight. She wants to go into assisted living. I realised the unnecessary sacrifices I've made were because I'm afraid I'll make you miserable, that you'll resent me for inhibiting you. The way I've sometimes felt as a carer.'

The news was everything he wanted to hear but it was tinged with the hurt of knowing that Jessie hadn't come to the decision herself. 'That's great, but why are you here? What has that got to do with me?'

He saw the smile fall from her lips and took a step back to put some distance between them so he could think clearly. When he was near her, when she was touching him, he couldn't think of anything except being with her, and circumstances now meant he had more than himself to consider.

'I love you, Cameron.'

'Yet that has never been enough for you to be with me.'

'That's not fair.'

He shrugged. 'It's the truth.'

'I've been in a horrible situation my whole life. Only you ever made it bearable. I've only ever wanted what was best for the people I love. I'm probably never going to change.'

Cameron mulled over what she was saying to him and he realised that the selfless decisions she'd made over the years, though not always warranted or wanted, still made her the woman he loved. To ask her to change was impossible. If she'd been the kind of person who would've put her wants ahead of his, or her sick mother's, needs he probably wouldn't love her half as much as he did.

'I know,' he said softly, gathering her back in his arms. 'So, what are we going to do?'

'Well, I hadn't thought beyond apologising to the man I love and hoping he'd take me back.' She was looking up at him with such expectation and faith he was powerless to resist another second.

'Hmm, well, he might need a few more dates for you to convince him…and to let him have a say in things every once in a while,' he teased, only to earn himself a playful slap on the arm. 'But there's always a place for you in his heart.'

He kissed her again, a slow, leisurely display of his love, because now they had all the time in the world.

EPILOGUE

'Thomas… Simon…can you put the football away before you get your clothes dirty? Thank you.' Jessie folded her arms and waited for the boys to finish playing. Goodness knew how they'd managed to find a football at the register office, but they'd managed it.

She couldn't be angry with them when they were so good together, as though they were blood. Thomas had accepted Simon into the family just as easily as he'd accepted her. It had been a whirlwind year, her life, and theirs, changing beyond all recognition—for the better.

Her mother had made the transition into a care facility and seemed all the happier for it. She had friends and hobbies which filled her time and she had a new spark about her.

It might have something to do with a certain Richard who resided there too and was never too far from her side when Jessie and Cameron visited. She was glad her mother had found someone too, they both deserved some happiness.

Once her mother had sold the house to pay for her care it was only natural for Jessie to move in with Cameron and Thomas. He'd asked her long before then, but she'd waited until her mother was settled before taking the next step herself. Cameron had been incredibly patient although, left up to him, they would have married last year, when he'd first proposed. He didn't want to waste any more time but Jessie had insisted they try living together first to make sure everyone was okay with the situation, including Thomas. She needn't have worried. Although there were moments when he found things difficult to handle, they managed, just like any other family.

With a stable home on offer for Simon, who had been living with a temporary foster family, it had been easier to get the green light on the adoption, although there had been endless paperwork and interviews to ensure it was the best environment for him. Thankfully, social services could see how much they could do for him too. He was now recovering well and attending the same school as Thomas. Both she and Cameron made sure to take time off so they could attend his follow-up appointments at the hospital, even though he had a different doctor now overseeing his progress.

Of course there were times when the loss of his parents became too much for him. But Jessie and Cameron made sure to talk about them often and kept their memory alive as much as possible for Simon so he wouldn't forget them.

Today, exchanging vows with Cameron was the last piece of the family jigsaw slotting into place.

'Can we go in now?' Thomas asked, pulling at his sapphire-blue tie, which matched his and his father's eyes.

'Yes, let's do this, boys.' With Thomas taking one arm and Simon taking the other, they made their way into the building and down the aisle to where her handsome husband-to-be was waiting for them.

They passed Ciara, Agnes, the social worker, and Jessie's mother, who were all smiling at the wedding party, enjoying the moment with them.

The registrar greeted everyone, then asked, 'Who here gives this woman away?'

The boys chorused, 'We do,' to a delighted audience before taking their seats in the front row.

Jessie faced Cameron, who was wearing a tailored navy suit and a smile as big as hers. Although they hadn't gone for a big church wedding, she'd still opted to wear a traditional white wedding dress, a thirties-style maxi with a fake fur wrap, and gypsophila in her hair. She wanted to look special for her husband as they embarked on their new life together.

'You look beautiful,' he whispered, taking her hand as she joined him, sending that familiar jolt of arousal she still felt whenever he touched her. She knew then that their love for one another would never die.

Whatever happened next, as they said

their vows Jessie knew she was pledging herself not just to Cameron but to Thomas and Simon, and their future together. Every decision from now on would be a family affair. She would never be lonely again.

* * * * *

If you enjoyed this story, check out these other great reads from Karin Baine

Single Dad for the Heart Doctor
Festive Fling to Forever
A GP to Steal His Heart
Wed for Their One Night Baby

All available now!